BRIDE DOLL

ELIZABETH NANCY JANSEN

AUTHOR ACADEMY elite

Published by Author Academy Elite
PO Box 43, Powell, OH 43065
www.AuthorAcademyElite.com

Identifiers:
LCCN: 2021904145
ISBN: 978-1-64746-739-5 (paperback)
ISBN: 978-1-64746-740-1 (hardback)
ISBN: 978-1-64746-741-8 (ebook)

Available in paperback, hardback, e-book, and audiobook

Book design by JETLAUNCH. Cover design by Albert Bastasa.

Dedication

I dedicate this book to my dear mother. She found joy in the simple things, like the fragrance of her favourite yellow roses. Mom devoted her life to loving her family, and I will cherish my memory of her forever.

Artist Anthony Welch

CONTENTS

Chapter 1:   November 16, 2008 1

Chapter 2:   Adele and Jacque 5

Chapter 3:   Etta and Owen 10

Chapter 4:   Monique..14

Chapter 5:   Monique Finds Her Sailor............................17

Chapter 6:   Flynn, Adele, and Jacque............................ 20

Chapter 7:   Monique, Etta, and Owen........................... 23

Chapter 8:   The Wedding Preparations 29

Chapter 9:   The Wedding Day....................................32

Chapter 10: Return to the Farm.................................... 36

Chapter 11: Monique Pregnant 39

Chapter 12: Lily 42

Chapter 13: Monique Pregnant Again 50

Chapter 14: Baby Number Two.................................... 54

Chapter 15: Monique and Psychiatry 59

Chapter 16: Monique in Toronto 64

Chapter 17: Hello Little Stranger 71

Chapter 18: Back to Toronto..75

Chapter 19: Lily, the Big Sister.................................... 79

Chapter 20: Nia Growing Up.. 86

Chapter 21: Nia Takes the Bus.. 89

Chapter 22: Nia, the Teenager 93

Chapter 23: Nia Goes to University................................ 98

Chapter 24: Engaged 103

Chapter 25: Here Comes the Bride..............................107

Chapter 26: Nia as a Mrs. 114

Chapter 27: Nia, a Mother... 119

Chapter 28: Infidelity 128

Chapter 29: Nia Learns to Play 134

Chapter 30: Nia Meets Fernando 139

Chapter 31: Maria and Carlos......................................144

Chapter 32: Wedding Number Two 147

Chapter 33: Apgar of One... 151

Chapter 34: Nia Gives Birth Again 156

Chapter 35: Nia Has Another Boy 158

Chapter 36: Autism 162

Chapter 37: November 16, 2008, Continued.................166

Chapter 38: Nia Hits Rock Bottom 170

Chapter 39: Nia Starts on Her Path of Recovery........... 172

Chapter 40: Does He Love Me? 178

Chapter 41: Nia Meets Arjan 181

Chapter 42: Nia's Disclosure 187

Chapter 43: Nia Finds Her Happy Ever After 191

Book Club Discussion Points 196

About the Author..197

You have just finished reading Bride Doll....................199

CHAPTER 1

NOVEMBER 16, 2008

N ia had delayed this well-rehearsed plan long enough. She couldn't bear one more week ending the same way it had for the last two years. She began executing her plan by having an early dinner that night. Nia took extra care to prepare a delicious prime rib dinner with all of the fixings for her husband, Fernando. She wanted it to be just right, knowing it would be her last loving gesture despite his all too familiar foul mood.

It was 5:30 p.m. Nia had her Jeep already packed with Mika's favourite books, Disney movies, and his portable DVD player. Nia also brought fifty tablets of his antipsychotic medication, a large bag of Smarties, and two cans of Coke. In the back of the vehicle, she kept her own stockpile of antipsychotic meds, including fifty antidepressant tablets for her. Her chaser was not going to be a can of Coke, though. She had her favourite 1.5-litre bottle of chilled white wine to soothe her during her hopeless and desperate plan.

Nia was well beyond her ability to endure one more sad day. At age thirteen, Mika was reluctant to get into the vehicle, knowing he would have to go back to his dreaded place, Children's Psychiatric Research Institute (CPRI).

"NO I, NO I, NO I," Mika desperately cried out to communicate emphatically using his extremely limited vocabulary.

This was his usual decry to returning to the place he hated. Nia knew what his reaction would be getting into the vehicle. Over the past months, she'd heard and felt his heart-wrenching cry to be rescued from that dreaded place. When she first heard his imploring words, she immediately recognized them as his attempt to find the right words, which sounded like "no-eye, no-eye"; it took her months to figure out he was saying, "NO I" as in the last letter of CPRI.

Mika aggressively and vehemently shook his head while pulling at Nia's face for her eyes to meet his. She needed to reassure him she understood his distress at returning to the place where he received residential treatment for his aggressive autistic behaviours. He had been there for two years, and he wasn't getting any better. Mika's hatred of the place negated the objectives of the treatment. Despite his high-level psychology team having identified this obstacle, there was nowhere else for this severely autistic teenager to go.

Every weekend, he was allowed a one-night leave of absence (a brief relief, from Saturday afternoon until Sunday after dinner). Mika loved to see his mom's Jeep drive up to his maximum-security building. Nia would see his sad face turn into a smile, and his shoulders would drop into a more relaxed state. As he entered the vehicle, he would begin his excited utterances well understood by only his mother, "I of you, ways ever" (I love you, always forever). He didn't have the language skills to convey to his mother all the things he thought and felt, but he could script his desire to reconnect with his mother. There was always a cataclysmic emotional storm in her gut as she picked him up. She missed her son, and she loved him so much. However, she needed the help of a team of health care professionals to find a way for him to decrease his destructive behaviours and be less of a threat to his family, others, and himself. It was terrible, and she knew it'd only get worse.

Upon arriving home with Mika, Nia's husband always retreated to the study. With the door firmly closed, he wouldn't have to listen to his son screaming—that would interfere with his televised hockey game. Sadly, her daughter was no longer living at home but with her grandmother. Isabella, only fourteen, couldn't cope with Mika's meltdowns and physical abuse. Nia had no other choice but to protect her daughter.

Nia didn't want to resort to having Mika confined to a residential behavioural treatment facility, but she'd exhausted all of her options. Mika was only getting worse, and he was a burden everywhere he went. His extended family avoided him out of fear. The pain was too great; Nia couldn't bear dropping him off at CPRI one more time. He was yelling "NO I" until Nia gently whispered in his ear, "No I." Mika stopped screaming, holding Nia's face close to his to validate with her words, her soft voice, and her tender smile. "No I."

Hand in hand, they went to the garage and got into the Jeep. Nia ensured Mika had his seat belt on before he could see what was packed in his backpack. As predicted and planned, he squealed in delight at all of his favourite things in the bag. Nia noticed Mika's hesitant looks as she drove down the street. She knew he was concerned about her turning in the familiar direction to the dreaded "NO I." Mika's face relaxed in relief as Nia turned in the opposite direction.

It was twilight; she'd rehearsed this camouflaged nightmare more times than she cared to recount. She drove to Lobo, a tiny village outside of London, Ontario, where there was a horse farm with an old abandoned barn to park in the back. Nia's friend, Bri, leased the pasture where her horses stayed outdoors for the winter. Nia knew no one except the animals would be witness to this homicide-suicide. The horses were unconcerned with her vehicle approaching and continued with their munching of hay. Nia turned off the Jeep while Mika cheerfully watched the horses.

Nia walked to the back of the vehicle for the bag with all she needed to complete the plan, including an old towel. She rolled the towel like a long tube and stuffed it carefully into the exhaust pipe. After taking her bag, she closed the back and got back inside the Jeep with her son.

Mika was happy to be with his mom, his Aladdin movie, his pop, and his Smarties. Nia cracked open the wine bottle and took long, purposeful gulps of the cool, delicious, familiar nectar of the serpent from hell. Yes, that was where she was most certainly going, but not her dear son; Mika would be rescued from his hellish life on earth. She leaned back, took another long drink of wine, and savoured the commencement of her happy place—being numb.

Nia's fingers reached toward the dangling keys. They almost reminded her of the mobile that danced above her children's cribs. Mika, who was happily absorbed in his cartoon, didn't hear the slight clang as her fingertips brushed against the keys. It took another sip of wine for the voice of warning to fade and replaced with the neutral feeling that accompanied going on a random errand. With a twist of her wrist, the engine came to life.

CHAPTER 2

ADELE AND JACQUE

Adele was not a beseeching woman; there was nothing demure about her or her vocation. She was the salt-of-the-earth-type of wife to a vegetable and animal feed farmer in Northern Ontario. The geographical location of this farming life required due diligence, giving real meaning to the phrase "make hay while the sun shines," as the growing season from thaw to harvest was only four months. Perhaps that's why she lived with defiant determination to see that the farm yielded the very best cabbages, cauliflowers, and hay in the region.

She was born in 1892 into a righteous Roman Catholic family from Sault Ste. Marie, Ontario. Adele was thought to be long past the marrying age at thirty-five when she met Jacque Gagne, who became a boarder in her family's home on Queen Street after WWI. Jacque was born in Montreal and moved to Massey, Ontario, at a young age with his family, who owned a 100-acre crop farm. Jacque joined the Canadian Army in 1915, and after an excruciating Army career—including being wounded three times—he became a well-decorated veteran, awarded the George Cross medal in 1917. The article in the Montreal newspaper identified Jacque as a Battalion runner displaying great courage during the operation of capturing Bellevue Spur in the battle of Passchendaele. Owing to a lack of communication except by runners, he repeatedly volunteered to carry messages. He passed through hostile barrages and heavy machine and rifle fire to deliver dispositions, showing absolute devotion to duty and complete disregard for his safety throughout the fighting. Because of his courageous behaviour, despite all difficulties, communication was maintained. There was no doubt that Jacque's descendants for generations to come would be hard-wired to be courageous.

Following the war, Jacque needed a wife to start a devoted Catholic family who would service his religion and farming life. Like his war career, marriage was understood to be one's duty to be a good Catholic. A marriage, and the subsequently required fornication, was only sacred in the eyes of the church if the intention was solely for procreation. The Church wouldn't grant a marriage without the promise of children. Conforming, Adele and Jacque adamantly believed that sex without marriage was a mortal sin and anything other than a sacramental union was unorthodox and unacceptable to God.

The spring wedding in 1925, for all intent and purpose, was rudimentary and uneventful. Jacque wanted the wedding understated and efficiently orchestrated. There was no fanfare in the ceremony held in the Our Lady of Good Counsel Church rectory.

Adele wore her tired-looking, dark coloured Sunday best dress with an almost-matching and not-so-tattered dark brimmed hat. Adele had lived through the war and didn't see a reason to spend good money on anything that couldn't be used multiple times. However, she did have a prudent bouquet of pink peonies—her favourite flowers from her mother's garden—tied up with the only extravagance of the whole ensemble: a long white satin ribbon.

As their commitment would have it, four children were born to Adele and Jacque. Monique was the eldest. Much to the couple's dismay, none of their offspring chose the religious vocational life. Traditionally, for such a church-fearing

Catholic family with four offspring, at least one of their children was groomed to enter the priesthood or convent. Having a priest or a nun in one's immediate family gave them an elevated social status in the community.

Adele was good at being a farmer's wife. She was highly focused on the crop yield and all it took to get the best quality vegetables to market, bar none. Her general approach to life was from the glass-half-empty perspective. All that was of any importance to her was money: earning it, saving it, and, yes, hiding it under her mattress. Inherently due to her wartime life experience, she never entrusted her hard-earned currency to a banking institution.

Unlike farming, mothering was not Adele's strong suit. She raised her children in the shadows of meeting the demands of agriculture in Northern Ontario. Affection for her children was sparse, unlike the abundance of devotion to her fields. It was Adele's cabbages, not her babies, that held her daily focus.

Adele and Jacque needed more farmhands to help grow their farm. They seized an opportunity offered by the Canadian government to sponsor immigrants from Latvia. These newcomers were obligated to work on the farm for one year to pay back the country's financial investment in their passage to Canada. After one year of farm labour, the immigrants were free to find employment and sponsor their family members to this new land of opportunity.

Jacque was kind-hearted to the Latvians and housed four men at a time under his roof (albeit in the veranda). Adele kept her family separated from the "foreigners" behind the veranda door, secured with a large butcher knife jammed into the door frame. While Adele was the prevailing provider for the farmhands, she began each day with her self-care.

Heavy footed, Adele would descend the stairs dressed in the house dress she had worn the previous day. (Wash day was on Mondays, and a clean house dress would start on Tuesdays; the garment had to last unequivocally until the following

7

Monday for washing). Jacque had the same regime with his farming clothes. One became familiar and unaffected by the subsequent body odours synonymous with farming life.

Adele developed diabetes in her adult life. Her daily ritual necessitated sterilizing her glass needle for her insulin injection procedure. While the needle pieces were boiling, she made her breakfast: two slices of perfectly toasted bread spread with bacon fat (despite having freshly-churned butter in the icebox) and a whole orange. She ate her breakfast methodically while rocking back and forth in her black rocking chair. The creaking of the chair rocking and her loose dentures clicking as she chewed made for an interesting harmony. Adele wore long, cotton (formerly white) stockings hoisted over her flabby thighs, held up with thick black elastics rather than fashionable garters.

When she finished her breakfast, her needle components were ready for the injection process. The icebox contained the multiple tiny glass ampules of insulin. After the top of the ampule was snapped off to expose the grey, permeable surface, the needle would draw up the clear substance. In the opposite thigh from the previous day's injection site, she'd pierce her skin and administer the dosage. Once the process was over, she pulled up her perpetually sagging stockings and proceeded with her chores of the day.

After his daily regime of waking at 6:00 a.m. to attend French Mass on Cathcart Street, Jacque took a brief moment to drink his instant coffee and eat two pieces of perfectly toasted bread—always buttered on the concave side of each slice. To top it off, homemade strawberry preserves were spread onto the warm, buttered toast. Following this delightful part of his day, he would go upstairs and change from his church clothes into his farming attire. His morning routine concluded with lighting his pipe in his truck before driving to the fields.

By noon, the farmhands would follow Jacque to the outdoor water hose attached to the pump house to scrub their hands before entering the kitchen for their expansive "le dejeuner." Their typical midday meal consisted of riced potatoes, boiled carrots, green beans, tomatoes, leaf lettuce, and green onions—all fresh from the garden—along with fried pork chops followed by freshly baked rhubarb pie and instant coffee.

A jar of Sanka was passed around to each well-fed man. Following a thirty-minute rest in the veranda, the men would proceed back outside to smoke before beginning their second and final shift of work.

After the noontime meal, Adele would rest in her rickety old chair and sing "Alouette, Gentille Alouette" while her daughters begrudgingly washed and dried the dishes. Perhaps Adele believed she displayed her love for her family by modeling service—the practical and functional aspects of living a farmer's life. Her primary duty was to produce a saleable commodity to pay the mortgage banker and the dreaded taxman.

The weather for Adele was the abominable boogie man to be feared each day, as it could have profound interference with the harvest. If it was too cold in the spring, the frost delayed the planting. Too much rain or not enough rain could destroy all of the crops. Adele wanted money, a viable farm, her husband, and her children (in that order).

CHAPTER 3
ETTA AND OWEN

Etta was the true Canadian version of the Victorian era, which explained her many social nuances, behaviours, and discernments. Her well-to-do family home in the east end of Sault Ste. Marie. In its time, it had an air of propriety and distinction. The need for absolute adherence to the British monarchy's code of conduct was the expectation of her parents, grandparents, and their preferred company. This boiled down to one simple thing: all issues were seemingly categorized as either acceptable or foreign. You were white and of English descent—Anglican—or not, well-heeled or not. The 'not' part of anything was sternly and strictly avoided.

Etta met Owen right after WWI. Owen courted Etta's older sister Elizabeth for a short period until he realized it was Etta for whom he truly felt love and a need to cherish. In 1925, after a fitly chaperoned courtship, they were married. The wedding was beautifully appointed, befitting a royal princess bride, and the accoutrements were exquisite. She had (of course) the traditional virgin white gown—an ankle-length gown, primly designed with a high Victorian neckline and long lace sleeves. The satin bodice and skirt of the dress had an overlay of lace to match the sleeves. The bridal accessories included white lace gloves and a fine pair of white leather tie-up boots with a small heel to elevate her petite five-foot frame. Her lace veil featured a delicate white satin tied bonnet that caressed her shoulders and flowed into a cathedral train behind her. Etta's traditional English bride bouquet consisted of a cascade of red roses and English ivy. She was truly a beautiful bride, entrancing Owen as she walked down the aisle of St. Luke's Anglican Church. Etta could tell she had made her parents proud with her choice in a husband. In her mind, she felt like she was a perfect princess bride as she held her father's arm. She proceeded with naïve confidence to meet her groom to the tune of the traditional Mendelssohn's "Wedding March" played by the old, crusty church organist.

Etta had attended many weddings with her parents over the years of her impressionable life, but her true model for a crowning marriage was her parents'. Her father didn't display overt affection for anyone. His purpose in life was to provide the necessities of a typical upper-middle-class family with discipline and good order for all those under his roof. Her mother rarely demonstrated endearment for her husband, as if it was distasteful or below her station to kiss and hug him, let alone her children. To Etta, daily marital relations between a husband and wife looked like pleasantries. "Good morning, Dear," while eating breakfast, followed by "Thank you, Dear. I trust you will have a lovely day," ending with "Good night, my Dear," as each of them retired to their separate bedrooms. The whole idea of actually doing "the deed" didn't titillate Etta in the least.

It was only a few days before the wedding when her mother gave her the Victorian version of how to do the sexual act necessary to consummate the marriage. In doing so, she conveyed the act of intercourse with the opaqueness of a wedding veil. Etta's take away from the teaching was that marital sex was something to submit to on the wedding night and as infrequently as possible thereafter. It was on this premise that she managed her matrimonial obligations.

Being one of the few privileged married ladies of that steel town, Etta had a multitude of beautiful dresses and a closet to rival any English-influenced woman in Canada. Her favourite dress shop was Sandy's on Gore Street. Every new season, Etta would bring home two new dresses to try on and keep them for a week to determine if she wanted to have both, one, or none. The store only offered this practice to the few high society ladies. The alchemy of attractiveness was in how Etta could stylize each outfit. Her high-heeled pumps always matched her handbag, as did her kid leather gloves. For this industrial municipality, she was the "cherry on top," and it was Owen's true delight as Etta's husband to gift her with all he could.

Owen loved to be playful with Etta. In response, she would scold him for his rogue behaviour, as if it was a nuisance to her. Despite her reaction, his favourite flirtatious display was to peek down her brassiere on the premise that he was checking to see if his fifty-dollar bill was still there. If not, he would have a replacement to tuck into her garment after a bounteous visual delight.

As emulated by her parents, Etta's indoctrinated belief was sex had only one purpose: to dutifully make her body available for a husband and wife encounter for the strict intention to impregnate. Therefore, her marital sleeping accommodations entailed separate bedrooms and remained this way throughout their union. Once Etta was with child, she had fulfilled her marital duty and chose never to endure such bodily displeasure again.

Flynn was born to Etta and Owen in March 1926. His childhood, by any other Sault Ste Marie comparison, was privileged, overly-protected, and indulged. Etta was resistant to Flynn meeting traditional forms of child development. For example, Flynn failed kindergarten twice because Etta only allowed periodic attendance, given that he would be susceptible to germs and likely the distasteful influence of poorly behaved children. The real reason for Flynn's absences was because she missed him too much to allow him to attend school. Despite all the hovering from his mother, Flynn became a tall, handsome, athletic, well-humoured, carefree man with every opportunity life could offer. His life was top shelf, which included a car at sixteen, a fast boat, and a camp on Squirrel Island. As fathers did at the time, Owen acquired work for his son in the same occupation as himself. Owen was a foreman at Algoma Steel, and when Flynn came of age at sixteen, he worked in his father's department.

At seventeen, Flynn enlisted into the Royal Canadian Navy and went to serve in WWII. Owen hid his need to shelter his son from his unforgettable experiences of the mud and blood survival in the trenches in WWI. Owen was relieved it was the Navy and not the Army that Flynn was pursuing. It was there, Flynn developed his life-long passion for sailing. His sailor experience was full of mischievous adventures, some of them being more serious, like going MIA and being put in the hull for not returning to the ship on time in Montreal. French girls were at the core of all of his naval misdemeanours, and, oh, how things changed, especially for Etta, when Flynn discovered French kissing.

CHAPTER 4

MONIQUE

Monique never fit the Gagne mould. It was a constant internal conflict for her to fit in while discovering her own aspirations and some degree of contentment. Monique, unlike her mother, Adele, lived with a "glass half full" mindset. As a result, Monique kept her imaginary world well-guarded within her reality.

Life on the farm compromised Monique physically, emotionally, and spiritually. She was a sickly child; it was a small wonder she didn't perish trying to fight off her many bouts of pneumonia attributed to the damp, cold, and draughtiness of the old farmhouse.

Having a life's purpose of growing cash crops was definitely not the path Monique wanted. Her interests were more abstract than the concrete essence of her mother's. Books, not shovels, were her tools. Doing her required daily chores on the farm, which consisted of hoeing, weeding, and picking, was a dreaded daily penance.

Despite her health issues, Monique was at the top of her class in her early academic life. At school, she found her niche: mathematics, biology, physics, and geography. Academia became her enlivened calling. She felt the mundanity of her simple life unbearably self-limiting. From an early age, Monique yearned for a more global reality. The farm and her mother were her unendurable anchors. Ironically, it was the diagnosis of asthma that released her from her bondage. Following the doctor's recommendation to move her from the farm environment, she was handed off to her father's spinster sister in Massey. There, Monique's academic life was encouraged and praised. She discovered new freedoms, and the barn door of her previous life was flung wide open; she was the beautiful black filly exploring greener pastures.

In Massey, following her secondary education, Monique's options and desires for continued academia were limited. Finances were the defining factor. Adele would only agree to Nursing School. Jacque and her grand-pere wanted her to go to McGill University in Montreal to continue feeding her passion for biology. Predictably, Adele put her heavy foot down, and so nursing it was. At least Monique didn't have to return to the farm. By continuing her education in Sault Ste. Marie, she had the intriguing experience of the somewhat "naughty life" of a nursing student's residential lifestyle. It didn't take long for Monique to established a duality to herself; by day, she fostered diligence to the sterility of the teachings of the Sisters of St. Joseph (the Order for Caring for the Sick). This was juxtaposed with the shenanigans of a revered nursing student delighting in evening impish escapades. Monique was the most beautiful and the most daring of her classmates, flaunting her exquisite beauty and innate French attributes and sensuality. She wasn't that shadow of a girl from the farm anymore; she was the "diva of the steel town" living up to and redefining the naughty nurse delight of many young men's imaginations.

The horizontal black velvet ribbon gracing her nursing caps' top rim signified her achievement of becoming a Registered Nurse. The highlight of her career was when she became an operating room nurse. Monique wasn't shy about being proud of her work. She felt dignified by the status of her qualifications.

Adele never told her daughter she was proud of her accomplishments. In truth, Adele was disappointed her eldest daughter didn't become a nun, as she secretly hoped that would be her hall pass to heaven.

Monique readily understood the science of nursing; it was the practical caring for the patients that was incongruous with her vocational path. Sputum, puke, and excrement were not her forte. It was her training rotation in the operating room that fascinated her. The sterilizing process of the surgical instruments was perfectly mastered. Her OR nursing technique was envied by her peers and praised by her teachers. Being an OR nurse, she didn't have to be skilled in bedside manner as her patients were anaesthetized. The surgeons would toss dice to win the OR suite Monique would be working in for the day.

She was a sight to behold. Even with her surgical mask on, her brown eyes radiated throughout the room. Monique seized her bewitching power over the surgeons. She knew her vivaciousness was like a drug to them.

CHAPTER 5

MONIQUE FINDS HER SAILOR

It was on one of the few hot and humid Saturday nights in Sault Ste. Marie when Monique and her nursing friend, Natalie, went to a dance at the Royal Canadian Legion. It was there that Monique unexpectedly met an unbelievably captivating sailor. She shocked even herself at how attracted she was to that healthy male specimen. Undoubtedly, he was the pin-up poster for a returned-from-war Canadian sailor-turned-steel worker. From Monique's perspective, he was certainly a person of interest on her Romeo radar.

Her dance card was already full, yet she knew the copulating frenzy of the jazz music fuelling the energy in the dance hall couldn't preclude her need to take action and clear some slots on her dance card. The subject of her gaze hadn't noticed her yet. Instead, a sleazy, bottled-blonde with a ridiculous ponytail was occupying his attention. Monique instinctually employed her sensual prowess by swaying to the music, which successfully gained his attention.

Monique had always been more intrigued by the sailors at Legion dances than the Army or Air Force guys. For that matter, they piqued her interest even more than the doctors from the hospital where she worked. She continued to sway with the music. Flynn turned around and leaned his back into the bar. Monique found his full-frontal gaze, and time stopped (but not the music). Her tall, exquisitely formed body was now of prime interest to this sailor. Flynn was clearly on her sea and sailing into a memorable Saturday night delight.

As if pulling in his mainsail, Flynn drew Monique into his mast-like frame before engaging in their first dance, the jitterbug. In the mood and groove, they danced until the end of the evening, much to the disappointment of the Army guys on her dance card, which was forgotten in her purse alongside her tube of red lipstick. They didn't stand a chance, as Flynn wasn't looking to surrender his captivating acquisition. Being a seasoned woman-seeker in different ports, Flynn felt this situation was different, fresh, and enticing.

A Sunday picnic at Harmony Bay followed the dance. The beach blanket emulated the dance floor; however, the posturing was horizontal on the beach. It was such a thrilling time for Monique; nothing seemed forbidden or conforming. Her free spirit sailed with her sailor's. Flynn's mainsail was taunting to catch the waves into Monique's heart. Without question, he desired the French woman. Her allure was unrelenting. Laughter and frolicking behaviour propelled her to feel ready to embrace her own satisfaction, being that sexy seductress who could so easily hook any stud she desired. Any hints of her farm-girl life were far removed.

The summer of 1952 embodied party after party, dance after dance, picnic after picnic, beach after beach, and their romance flourished. Despite her comfort with her sensual ooze, Monique hadn't been intimate with a man before. On the other hand, Flynn had had multiple sexual encounters throughout his naval life but never had truly made love to a woman. Monique was his first "special" sexual experience. She held nothing back from his warm arms and hungry kisses. Without hesitation, Flynn was a "man overboard" and found himself swimming to Monique's shoreline with abandonment.

Over the summer, the two lovers traveled many robust seas, each more gratifying than the last. Flynn was consumed by his French woman, despite what his mother might think, and he wanted to seal her in his vault; a proposal transpired.

CHAPTER 6

FLYNN, ADELE, AND JACQUE

The lightning rods on the top of the farmhouse were no defence for the storm-of-all-storms that was about to pass over Adele and Jacque's farm. Monique was already trembling, and Flynn did the only thing he knew how to do—keep the sails taut and hold the course.

Flynn's car proceeded down Folk's Road—a distinctive tall corridor of evergreens framed the driveway that led the way to the old farmhouse. Inside, Adele was vigorously rocking in her chair, and Jacque was inhaling deeply on his pipe. Monique's brothers had long since headed for the barn to avoid the anticipated hailstones. Adele didn't like surprises. All Jacque and Adele knew about Flynn was he was "different," as conveyed by their second oldest daughter, who was already properly wedded. These were not comforting words to this bedrock couple.

Monique opened the door into the kitchen with Flynn's hand firmly in hers, giving a visual indication to her parents that this was her person of significance. "Mom, Dad, this is my fiancé, Flynn." Her statement was followed by a long, draughty pause of pending anxiety for all. True to character, Adele immediately started to ask the direct questions.

"Flynn; that's a different name. Are you from town?"

"Yes," Flynn said.

"What's your last name?"

"Kross."

That's certainly not a French name, Adele thought. "Where do you live?"

"On Simpson Avenue."

That must be a snobby east end address, definitely not in the farming area, she thought. "What are your parents' names?"

"Etta and Owen," Flynn replied.

Those aren't French names either, Adele declared in her mind. "What does your father do?"

"He is a foreman at the Algoma Steel Plant."

Hmm, don't know anyone who works at the plant except Aunt Margaret's neighbour, the Italian. "Where do you work?" Adele demanded.

"I served in the Royal Canadian Navy, and now I work at the plant with my father."

Well, he's handsome enough; Monique did well for herself there. He has a lean, muscular body; he'll make a fine farmhand for haying, she thought, while sizing up the young man in front of her. "What Parish do you and your family belong to?"

"Mrs. Gagne, my parents and I attend St. Luke's."

That was the first nuclear crack. Monique's quivering was becoming visually apparent.

"Mom, I love Flynn, and we're going to be married," Monique declared.

"But Monique, he isn't Catholic."

"Mom, Flynn is everything to me."

"Monique, he isn't Catholic," Adele repeated herself more forcefully.

"Dad, help me," Monique pleaded.

Jacque only inhaled deeper on his pipe.

"Monique, he isn't Catholic; you'll be committing a mortal sin. You must go to confession and beg for forgiveness, and you will need to do penance for your thoughts and actions."

"Mom, I am going to marry Flynn, and that is that," Monique said emphatically.

"Monique, the Commandments state you must honour your Mother and Father. Have you forgotten that? You will go to hell, and your children will be marred as retribution from God for your mortal sin."

"Dad, help me," Monique begged following her mother's emotional beating. The room was dense with pipe smoke and fury.

Flynn looked panicked and confused. "Monique, let's go. I want to go. Now. Goodbye, Mr. and Mrs. Gagne," he said as they hurried out the back door.

Flynn couldn't wait to get them both in the car and steered westward. He didn't care to ever return to the farm. He had never experienced such a family conflict. Flynn had a feeling their announcement wouldn't be easy. His planned strategy to turn on his candour and charm had failed him.

In the car, Monique's tears transformed from drips to sea swells. "Oh Flynn, what are we going to do? I knew this was going to be hard. I knew my father wouldn't intervene." Her father's silent anger etched a crater in her heart.

CHAPTER 7
MONIQUE, ETTA, AND OWEN

"Hi, Mom. Hi, Dad. I would like you to meet my beautiful Monique," Flynn said as he led his fiancée into the properly appointed English parlour.

Owen held his cigarette in his left hand while extending his right hand to Monique. His grip was gentle, warm, and friendly. Monique felt calm, even if it was only for a few seconds.

On the other hand, when Etta tried to follow suit and extended her hand, it was stiff and cold. She quickly tried to divert her attention.

"Son, are you hungry? You must be hungry. Let me fix you a roast beef sandwich. Monique, I will make you a cup of tea." Etta was relieved to escape the parlour.

Monique found herself admiring Flynn's home. There was a calmness and cleanliness, giving it a distinctive sense of order. She was relieved there was no evidence of farm clutter or stench from the barn. Monique silently laughed to herself and quickly redirected her olfactory sense to the aroma of the sweet floral fragrance of Etta's perfume.

Etta was impatiently waiting for the kettle to boil while Flynn was well into his sandwich with a smile on his face. He looked like he'd relaxed back into being in the comfort of his home. Monique was in the living room with Owen discussing the weather. "April showers bring May flowers," Etta heard Owen say cheekily and then heard him light another Export A. She returned to the parlour with a plastic tray (not the sterling) and presented the tea in the everyday bone china cup and saucer. (Not her good bone china, as that was only for high society company.)

Flynn paused in the kitchen to grab a beer from the icebox before joining the others in the parlour. He'd taken off his tie and pulled his shirt free from his belted pants while his shoes remained under the kitchen table.

Monique could feel her tension lessen as she focused on Flynn's air of outrageous sexiness. His dark, wavy hair fell over his forehead, and the downiness of his chest teasingly appeared at the crest of his unbuttoned shirt.

"By the way, Mom and Dad, Monique and I are planning to get married. We're thinking about May fifth."

Oh, how Monique didn't want a repeat of the previous parental disclosure. She squeezed her hands around the teacup and tried to ignore the thumping sound in her ear. Just as Flynn didn't meet her parent's expectations, she knew she wasn't going to be the exact prediction for a daughter-in-law for the Kross family.

"Son, are you sure?" Etta blurted out, making Monique squirm while holding her teacup.

"Yes, Mom, we're getting married soon."

This wasn't the response Etta wanted. "Why so soon, Son? We've just barely met your girlfriend. Owen, what do you think?"

Owen passively watched the conversation and took another long drag before blowing out a long stream of cigarette smoke.

Etta didn't wait for his answer. "Son, we don't know anything about this girl, and now you say you're going to marry her. I don't understand. I don't like the rush." Etta's flushed cheeks were the shade of her red lipstick, and she was desperate to have someone—anyone—agree with her. "Owen, what do you think? Son, you mustn't do this so quickly. What will our friends think? What's really going on here? My church auxiliary group will have no time to prepare. This just isn't going to work. Son, you must take all of this into consideration. You're our only child; we need to do this in an orderly manner. Son, are you listening? Owen, Owen, do you hear me?"

It became apparent to Monique how Flynn managed his mother's distress: with playful jesting. "Well, mother, you won't have to have the old buzzards over for tea to discuss your soon-to-be daughter-in-law's beauty and the contents of her hope chest." (Flynn had no idea what was in a hope chest; he'd only heard about such things from his mother's reference to her lady friends' daughters' wedding preparations.)

"Why, Son, why? I have looked forward to this day," she lied. "We've been to all of our friends' children's weddings. Remember how beautiful Madge's daughter looked walking down the aisle at St. Luke's? The organist played the same music Queen Elizabeth had for her walk down the aisle. I just will not have it, Son. You leave me no choice. Why must you hurt me like this? Owen, what is wrong with you? Tell your son this isn't right. Tell him."

Owen remained coolly holding his cigarette, and replied, "Etta, this isn't your wedding, nor is it one of our friends' family weddings. Flynn has made it very clear what he wants. I would like to know more about you, Monique. Let's not rush by putting the cart before the horse. Monique, would you like a rum and Coke? Son, can I fix one for you too? Etta, can I make a gin for you? Would you like tonic?"

She was quick to reply, "No tonic."

Owen retreated to the kitchen to make the drinks, grateful for the few moments to be free of Etta's emotional display of shame and impropriety.

Etta removed the freshly pressed hanky neatly tucked into her white brassiere she wore under her fashionable lady's afternoon dress. She patted her brow and took pause with the intolerable situation. Her thoughts begin to race. *Who is this girl? Why is my son interested in her? She doesn't have blonde hair or blue eyes like the girl I always thought Son would settle down with. She's too tall, too skinny, and doesn't dress like a fashionable English woman; she looks like a foreigner. I don't like the colour of her dress. Son doesn't like brunettes. Why her? Why would Son pull this on me? This can't be happening. I just won't let this nonsense continue.*

All these thoughts transcended simultaneously into a mass of confusion and frustration for Etta.

"Monique, I hope you like your cocktail the way I have mixed it," Owen said happily as he returned with the drinks.

Etta noticed—with dismay—he used his company cocktail glasses. *Why isn't he as pissed off as I am?* she muttered to herself.

"Monique, do you live around here?" Owen asked.

"No, I live in the Nurses Residence at the General Hospital," Monique replied.

Etta visibly cringed as she heard it was the Catholic Hospital. As a good Protestant, Etta had never set foot in the General Hospital. *Nothing but Dagos there*, she pompously declared to herself in silence.

Owen inquired, "So, you're a nurse?"

"Yes, an OR nurse."

Etta let out an audible gasp. *This is definitely unacceptable for Son's girlfriend to work in that Dago hospital. Really? Son thinks he's is going to marry a Catholic? Over my dead body.*

Monique gratefully sipped her rum and Coke, taking brief comfort in the niceties of Flynn's world while entirely oblivious to the scathing conversation happening inside Etta's mind.

"Monique, can you tell us more about yourself? What school did you go to?" Owen asked.

Etta silently pleaded to the universe. *She had better not be one of those DP's.*

"I did my second form in Massey," Monique replied.

There are only those Pea Wobblers in Massey. Oh my God, this girl is my worst nightmare. Son deserves better than this; he is better than this. Etta's gin was generously flowing down her strained throat.

"Ok, Mother and Dad, enough of the questioning. Monique and I would like to tell you about our actual wedding plans."

Etta shuddered from within. *By God, I am not going into a Catholic Church.*

"Mother, we're going to be married on May fifth at the city hall. Teddy and Vivian will be our witnesses," said Flynn.

Etta continued to feel exasperated. *I am* not *going to be seen with any damn DP farmers. That will never happen.*

"Mother, you don't look pleased," said Flynn.

"Son, I'm not. Owen, say something. He must not go through with this. Son, you're going to kill your mother if you do this. Have you thought this crazy idea through? Any children of yours will *not* be raised Catholic," Etta said with purpose and conviction.

Monique started to tear up while Owen remained passive and lit another cigarette.

In response and discord with his mother, Flynn said, "Mother, we will be going now. Monique, here is your coat."

Monique didn't hesitate and quickly pulled on her red car coat as she headed for the door. In quick pursuit, Flynn's large frame served as a barrier between his future bride and his irate mother.

Monique burst into sobs as Flynn opened the car door for her to slide in. As the door closed, he felt for the first time that this might be the opportunity to drop Monique off at her residence for good and take heed from his mother. Fear was creeping into his thoughts. He hadn't expected these feelings of confusion and cold feet.

Flynn started the engine and drove south on Simpson Avenue, heading toward the nursing residence. The two sat in silence, feeling overwhelmed and distraught. Both were independently sensing a fragmentation of their proposed union, as both sets of parents vehemently opposed it. This was the beginning of the crack in the foundation of their love and commitment to each other.

Monique got out of the car and walked with slumped shoulders toward the residence hall. She looked woefully back at Flynn as she closed the heavy door. Flynn sped off without even waving goodbye.

CHAPTER 8

THE WEDDING PREPARATIONS

Monique's friend, Vivian, rushed to greet her at the door. "Hi, how did it go? Did your parents just love Flynn? Did his parents fall all over you with happiness? They would be crazy if they didn't. Let's go shopping tomorrow; Sandy's has a snazzy pink suit in the window. I'm sure they'll have a wonderful hat to go with it. Monique, what's wrong? Snap out of it, girl. You're getting married," Vivian said with gleeful naivety. "Monique, really? Let's celebrate with a drink. Rum and Coke?"

The only word that could come out of Monique's mouth was "yes." She took the drink, gulped it down, and prayed it would numb her to sleep.

Monique and Vivian went to Sandy's dress shop after their respective shifts at the hospital. It had been only one day, and neither Flynn nor she had called each other. Monique settled herself by deciding it was often the case when Flynn was on the three to eleven-shift.

By three-thirty, Monique and Vivian were on the Queen Street bus on their way to Gore Street. As Vivian had described, the pastel pink suit displayed in the window was certainly an eye-catcher. Monique could feel her mood lighten as she entered the store and asked to try the outfit on. The size eight suit fit her perfectly. Monique continued to feel better as she found the perfect matching pink pillbox hat. She knew she could add some white veiling to it to pair with her white gloves, purse, and shoes.

Hints of excitement started to return as Monique looked in the mirror, acknowledging her glamour and elegance. She did love the suit; however, it was no wedding dress. A pink suit had never been in her girlish dreams of her wedding. There was supposed to be a long cathedral aisle, like the one at Precious Blood, for her bridal walk holding her father's arm. She had long dreamed of being draped in an abundance of white lace, peering behind a translucent veil while visualizing the overwhelming adoration in her soon-to-be husband's eyes. Her dreams of an epic wedding were going to be drastically compromised by the plain, inevitable courthouse wedding.

Monique's younger sister had a beautiful, traditional Catholic wedding one year prior. Attention was paid to every detail. Her husband came from meager means, but he was a good practicing Catholic, and that was his golden ticket to marrying her sister. Unlike his future brother-in-law, Flynn didn't have any acceptance or value (other than his strong back for haying time) in the Gagne family.

Flynn hadn't called Monique in four days. It was only two days till the wedding. In Monique's mind, there was a major civil war in play. The timeless pervasiveness of the battle between Catholics and Protestants, the French and the English, seemed like a continuous bad movie of discord giving her a migraine. Despite both being raised in a small Northern Ontario town, the streets defined the rigid boundaries of class, religion, language, and status.

Monique had unyielding anxieties about literally going to hell and only creating bastards. Purgatory for her future children was a taunting nightmare. However, when her thoughts returned to Flynn, her innate needs and desires overshadowed the ills of her mother's rant and rage.

Flynn felt restlessness, irritable, and discontent because of his mother's boldness to want to sabotage his choice of a wife. Where was the map to guide his future journey? Flynn realized he had lost his internal compass when it had come to Monique and marriage. "Is this a risk worth taking?" he repeatedly asked himself. Despite the reservations and the pressure of his mother's dismay and disappointment in his choice of a wife, he missed Monique's sensual teasing, naughtiness, and her hungry wanting of his embrace. It was easy for him to find himself longing for his soon-to-be bride.

In an attempt to distract and delay his decision to marry, Flynn filled his week with his default activity of play. In doing so, he was able to disassociate from the defining choice he had to make. There was seemingly no logic in this impending journey of his life. Providing for and protecting had never been a necessity beyond his deceased hunting dog called Jigger.

Bowling and beer filled the slipping of time before the wedding. He oscillated between "I do" and "I don't." Flynn and his mother never in his life had disagreed on anything major. He hadn't under any condition seen the look of angry horror in his mother's eyes. Flynn knew in his heart he had never hurt his mother like this before, not even with him going off to serve his country. At the very least, war was an honourable position, yet in his mother's eyes, this marriage was deplorable.

Needless to say, it was a restless night for Flynn. In his naïvity, he decided to make this life decision in the morning.

On the other hand, Monique was all alone in her room at the residence, fretting about the day to come and the lack of communication with her husband-to-be.

CHAPTER 9

THE WEDDING DAY

On the morning of her wedding day, she woke with a newfound inner direction, a purpose, a soulful decision (based on an eternal heartfelt love) to carry forward with her mission to marry Flynn. She made herself a strong coffee and proceeded to her happy place—the bathtub—where she washed away any remnants of self-doubt. To celebrate, she pleasured herself beneath her sea of fragrant bubbles.

By 9:00 a.m., Monique was off to her hair appointment for her signature brunette waves. She was quite pleased with her sleek, French flair and knew she would be a "knockout" on her wedding day. She returned to her residence room and enjoyed another strong cup of coffee and some cinnamon toast. Monique's hands were always well tended to, as was her hair. Applying hand lotion was her daily ritualistic passageway to her daydreams involving flowering meadows of love and her instinctual wilds.

Flynn ate his mother's usual prepared bacon and eggs breakfast with a cup of tea. There was no morning chit chat about how the day was about to unfold. In truth, Flynn was only following his destiny one minute at a time. The final showing up (or not) was yet to be decided. He showered, rubbing himself briskly with his Old Spice soap on a rope. He prolonged the hot water beating on his body until the water began to cool. His body quickly turned cold, signifying two things; the hot water tank had emptied, and decision time loomed.

Unlike Flynn, Monique was savouring the moments of her bridal preparations. She adored the feel of her new white, French-imported silk brassiere and panties with a matching lace garter belt to attach her skin-toned sheer stockings. Monique took great care with donning her hosiery, ensuring not to snag them and that the seams were perfectly straight up the back of her long, perfect legs. Her exquisite lingerie now served her in a supposititious manner, allowing her to feel magnificently attired for her wedding—despite not having her much dreamed about traditional, cathedral lace wedding gown and veil. She paused in front of the full-length mirror in her delicates, wanting to hold on to the image of her beauty. Proceeding with her dressing and viewing in the mirror, she acknowledged how well she carried herself in her pink wedding clothes and hat, matched with white gloves, high heels, and a beaded purse. She truly felt fit for the cover of the Vogue Paris magazine. Finally, she was ready. With grace, freedom, and determination, she proceeded to the front entrance of her residence.

Flynn was driving up to the circular drive. He'd taken the keys to his father's new Ford. Monique's greeting smile was radiant and outshone the lustre of the new car's paint. Flynn stepped out of the car to open the door for his magnificent beauty.

There was no conversation on the way to the City Hall; the warmth of their hand-holding was all the reveal needed to proceed with their quest. The ceremony was brief, but the wedding kiss was long. Flynn maneuvered his bride back to the borrowed gem on four wheels and proceeded east on Queen Street. He turned left onto Simpson Avenue, blowing his horn in triumph.

Etta's heart was wailing inside when she heard the horn blowing. She had prepared small sandwiches and scones with Devonshire cream for high tea. To match this menu, she displayed it on her mother's Spode tiered plates. When Flynn left with his suit on, she knew the foreboding outcome. She felt her prayers were unheard, so she resorted to silent rage with planned retribution for this unwanted act.

Owen wore his tailored suit jacket and pants with his brogues and fedora tilted just right to the side. He greeted his new daughter-in-law with a gentle, warm handhold as she exited the Ford. Owen knew when he heard his car rumbling in the morning that Flynn would be returning with his bride.

The overt posturing of being civil transpired with Etta's speechless unwelcoming of her new daughter-in-law. After the nicely presented luncheon, Flynn and Monique got in their own "our car" and raced down the highway to Niagara Falls on their Mr. and Mrs. Honeymoon.

Their pre-wedding awaiting dilemmas appeared even smaller in their review mirror. Somewhere near Massey, the married couple drove up on a small encampment along the highway. A bed was all they desired as Flynn flung open the doorway, carrying his bride like a hunter's prize.

Standing her alongside the closed door, he revelled in her sheer exquisiteness. He took his sweet time to kiss the skin beneath each unbuttoning, savouring her soft, wild rose-scented skin. Monique lavished in his heated kisses against the cool door.

Flynn loved her long neck, surrendered in radiant beauty. Monique's pink suit jacket gently dropped onto the old wooden floor, the skirt easily unzipped, and she stepped out of it, leaving the long, lanky legs illuminated by the lustre of her fine French hosiery. As they embraced, Monique could feel the bonding to Flynn intensify as their bodies united in marital beauty and passionate bliss.

Flynn hadn't expected Monique to up her game in her sexual prowess following their wedding. At that moment, he was blindsided by how extensive his new wife's intimacy and ability to make love had evolved. Monique was a far cry from any other he'd known. She owned her passion.

CHAPTER 10

RETURN TO THE FARM

One week later, the honeymoon came to an abrupt end as the Ford turned off Folk's Road and onto the sparsely gravelled lane. Giant evergreen trees cast their shade along the statuesque corridor that led to the farm. As Monique graciously stepped out of the Ford, she noted her precious lily of the valley and forget-me-not flowers covering the earth below the magnificent trees, swaying ever so subtly in the wind.

Anticipating the visit, Adele asked Jacque to stay behind with her at the farmhouse after his lunch and ritual smoking of his pipe. Breaking his routine and not returning to the field after his lunch break was irritating for Jacque.

Monique led the way into the kitchen. "Hi, Mom and Dad." The evidence of a massive lunch was still on the table. Monique gestured to Flynn to sit down and handed him a clean plate and a coffee mug. A slice of rhubarb pie awaited him. Monique's hands had a slight shaking (noticed by Adele) as she poured the boiling water over the scooped instant coffee in the mug.

Taking a deep breath, Monique declared, "Mom, Dad; Flynn and I got married a week ago."

A raging silence consumed the room for several minutes. Finally, Adele bellowed, "What?" She scowled as she gathered the dishes from the table. "Jacque, this can't be happening. Monique, this is a mortal sin. I was afraid of this happening, Monique. I raised you better than this. Jacque, your daughter is going to hell. Jacque, she will be excommunicated. Monique, how could you shame yourself and your family? He is a deplorable Anglican, and we are Catholics. You were raised to know better."

Flynn looked at his bride as she was trying to muster up the strength of a warrior woman to protect herself and her new husband from the wrath. At that moment, Flynn's only strategic alignment with Monique was to drink the instant coffee and eat the pie.

Monique was deep in the battlefield with her parents and their carved-in-stone beliefs. She was not trying to change them; she was only seeking love and acceptance for herself and her cherished husband. Fundamentally, she knew she was only deluding herself by delaying the inevitable war tactics.

"You are living the life of a whore now, and your babies will all be bastards. The Church will never recognize this marriage. You will be excommunicated. You foolish girl." Adele's words got more powerful and more demeaning with each breath.

As the ugly words continued to be torpedoed, Monique's face displayed her reality of powerlessness over her mother's convictions.

Jacque didn't intervene; he didn't have to—the expression on his face expressed his disdain. His anger disconnected him from his heart as a direct result of Monique's actions of defiance.

Flynn could take no more. "Monique, we are leaving right now." Flynn had reached his limits of tolerance for the implosion of his new family alliance.

The situation visibly shook Monique to her core. She followed her husband, retreating from the war zone back to the safety of their car. The fresh war wounds pervasively cast darkness over Monique, her marriage, and her future children. Her parents were right; she'd ex-communicated herself before God and the Church. Monique's trembling made her inconsolable.

Flynn once again found himself on foreign territory like a sailor lost in a desert storm.

Without question, he had witnessed the cracking of his new bride. Their fresh wedding vows and shining gold rings untethered from the verbal blasting.

Her mother's word of "ex-communication" was now etched in her mind. Monique knew this wouldn't be a pleasant task to inform her parents of her new marriage, but the defilement of her union was defeating her. Monique had no defence except to cave in her parents' contempt.

The drive home to their adorable, furnished one-bedroom apartment Owen had found for them on Aries Avenue (one block from his parents' and far away from the farm) was in silence. It was during that drive that Flynn felt the joy of their union dissolve. Flynn, in his naivety, thought the splendour would last forever.

Monique never saw her parents in a favourable light again. They had intentionally made her an outcast. As a result of betraying them and their faith, she felt emotionally ill to her core. Flynn's parents would see his French exotic and erotic bride now wore the cape of a marred woman. Her fire within now only faintly smouldered. She had crossed the foreboding religious line of Catholics into what was believed to be the no man's land of the devil himself. She knew this wasn't finished just with ex-communication; there would be further punishments.

CHAPTER 11
MONIQUE PREGNANT

Too tarnished and preoccupied with sin to practice any consistency of adherence to the Pope's newly sanctioned form of birth control, the Rhythm Method, Monique was pregnant by early June. Unfortunately, there was no delight in this. Flynn never really fully entertained the idea of becoming a father (likely because he never really gave up on being a carefree teenager). Monique became more destabilized with each passing day by her mother's etched designation of "bastards."

Relentlessly, Monique had to repair the damages of her choices. The mortal sin of marrying outside of the Catholic Church had to be rectified at all costs. It had to be done before their child was born a bastard and would live the life of an ousted child, spending his or her afterlife in purgatory. A lifetime of catastrophic consequences ruminated in all aspects of Monique's obsessive thoughts.

Flynn, just shy of thirty, didn't feel ready for this degrading development in his bilateral parental casting of shame. Although forewarned, he didn't fully appreciate the triad of hostility from Monique's parents, his parents, and his wife until he was deep within it. Life was so simple when his mistress was the sea. His life was now locked "in irons."

More choices had to be made. Monique wouldn't give rest until her need to have their marriage blessed was complete.

Conversely, Etta and Owen emphatically wanted to raise Flynn's children Anglican and to discredit all acknowledgement of Monique's French-Canadian heritage. Flynn was so uncomfortable in all aspects of this life-altering dilemma. His only reprieve was to join an Algoma Steel Plant bowling league.

Monique left her duties at the hospital, given that she was pregnant and rightfully incapable of caring for anyone other than herself. Her already limited compassion for her patients had left her. Monique was utterly consumed with her "sin," just as Adele had prophesied. Flynn had no defences against this invasive phenomenon infecting their marriage.

It was the ferocious and simultaneous battles between the Catholics against Anglicans, the French against English, Adele against Etta, Adele against Monique, and Etta against everything relating to Monique. Their life of conflicting absolutes had to change. Monique needed to extinguish her obsession with being "ex-communicated," if only for the wellbeing of their baby.

Flynn finally consented to have their marriage "blessed," which meant an absolution of their civil union and re-marrying in the Lady of Good Counsel's rectory. Predictably, the priest was irritated by Monique's choices but finally agreed to a Catholic "blessing" to be held October thirty-first. The date was a permanent reminder of her reprehensible choices. Monique left the church rectory feeling relieved, but not revived, while Flynn felt violated by the regimens of the opposing Christian religion. The only good that came out of their backdoor ceremony was they now had a legitimate Catholic marriage.

Monique, like her mother, hated being pregnant. The unpleasantness of morning puking, fatigue, and an expanding belly prevailed her thoughts. Flynn could only get her to smile when he brought her home a cherry blossom chocolate treat after bowling.

Adele only called their apartment when Jacque needed help on the farm. She didn't want to see her pregnant daughter. Adele still wanted to punish her daughter for compromising the Gagne family in the eyes of the Church.

When Monique went into labour, Flynn secretly followed his mother's direction and took her to the Protestant hospital. (The Plummer Hospital was directly beside The General Catholic hospital in the small steel town.) Etta wouldn't have her first grandchild born in the "Dago hospital." She wouldn't be able to handle the shame within her circle of firmly planted Protestants.

Dutifully, Flynn waited until the last possible moment, when Monique was deep into labour and begging for ether, to drive from the General Hospital parking lot to the Plummer Hospital Emergency Department to have their baby delivered.

CHAPTER 12

LILY

Lily was born an absolute brown-eyed beauty. She amazed her parents and delighted Etta and Owen to no end—a real treasure was gifted on that day. Monique's smile reappeared from its long hibernation.

Flynn felt fear and joy simultaneously. Later that evening, Flynn called the farm out of duty and asked to speak to Jacque. "Hello, Sir, this is Flynn. Monique and I now have a healthy baby girl."

Before Flynn could convey the infant's name, Jacque uttered "ok" and hung up the phone on the kitchen wall. Jacque was heading to the pumphouse, where he kept his homemade wine. He had to keep up the façade of contempt in front of Adele as he passed her rocking fiercely in her old rocking chair. "It's a girl." Once he got to the pumphouse, he filled one of the old, scratched juice glasses to the brim and lit his pipe. In his solitude, he allowed himself to feel joy for his grandbaby. In delight far removed from Adele, he sipped and puffed in his subdued secret celebration.

Being a mother was not a natural fit for Monique. The foreboding aspect of having a baby only grew out of the deeply embedded fear that her baby would suffer "the wrath of God" for marrying outside the Catholic Church. Monique checked her baby girl many times over to ensure she was anatomically correct. Baby Lily was not only a perfect creation, but she was also exquisitely beautiful. As it was the norm in the 1950s, mothers stayed in the hospital for ten days. Despite being both horrified and mortified that Flynn brought her to the Plummer Hospital, she was grateful her baby was safely delivered. For those divine days, she had ample rest to readjust to her non-pregnant self.

After an uninterrupted night of sleep and following her last breakfast in her hospital bed, Monique read the Sault Star. Flynn had dutifully (as orchestrated by Etta) placed the birth announcement in the paper. Lily Ann, seven pounds and ten ounces, proud parents Monique and Flynn Kross, and grandparents Etta and Owen Kross. Notably, the Gagne's were omitted from the birth announcement. Flynn was oblivious to the birth announcement etiquette and wrote it as his mother dictated. Monique chose not to react to this error; she didn't want anything to disturb her well deserved rest after pushing out the Kross bundle of joy.

Etta and Owen were over the moon with their brown-eyed beauty. Every evening, the pair would visit the hospital nursery and gaze through the window at the row of bassinets. The big pink card with the name Kross identified their treasure. The white beaded wrist bracelet with the corresponding name peaked out from the swaddled babe.

Monique was relieved when she was told her milk was too thin, and it was much better to have the baby on formula (this was the message to all mothers during these years). As expected by the maternity ward routine, Monique walked to the nursery at 10:00 a.m. She quietly rocked her baby while the infant sucked on her three-ounce bottle of warm formula, followed by the rhythmic, gentle patting of Lily's back for the much-anticipated baby burp. After twenty minutes, as Monique was about to get up from the rocking chair, the surly nurse told her to burp her baby again. Without discussion, Monique gave an arrogant stare to the attending nurse and handed her baby over, convinced she was too tired to stay any longer.

During Monique's hospitalization, Flynn moved back into his parent's home, readily resuming his "son" position in the family. Without missing a beat, Flynn was soothed to be under his mother's care, if only for a brief time.

Flynn was proud to pick up his beautiful wife, who looked rested and well-coiffed. Her signature red lipstick enhanced her glow. He met her at the hospital's front door as the porter helped her stand from the wheelchair with her babe in arms. Flynn opened the car door for his new little family. The porter handed Flynn the standard departure bag of three hospital prepared bottles of formula.

Etta had meticulously prepared their apartment for her new granddaughter. Two dozen white flannel diapers—freshly washed and folded, of course—with pink diaper pins, pink plastic diaper pants, one dozen white diaper shirts, six baby blankets (pink, of course); the whole list Monique created while in the hospital was delivered with tender loving care.

Owen cleaned the new parents' apartment until everything shone. Both happily fatigued, Etta and Owen looked in awe at each other, still unable to believe their son was now a dad. They quickly closed the door behind them and silently drove home, leaving Flynn and Monique to their privacy when they arrived at their family address.

"Ah, how nice of your parents. Everything looks so clean and organized, I must thank them." (Monique knew she never would.)

Predictably, with a new baby and a husband working shift work, finding a peaceful and orderly course of a day became a foreign concept. Monique felt her mind, body, and soul were on a hormonal rampage within herself. Relying on her nursing background and baby care refresher teaching while in the hospital, Monique put her baby Lily on a strict bottle-feeding regime every four hours. Like clockwork, baby Lily would start crying at three hours. It was Monique's firm belief not to feed the baby until the exact scheduled time. "It's supposed to be good for babies to cry," she repeatedly told Flynn. However, baby Lily cried inconsolably, frequently throughout the day and night.

By the fourth day home, the new little family had already begun its etchings of fragmentation. Flynn panicked when he arrived back at their apartment. Immediately, he heard the baby inconsolably crying once again. Monique was in the bedroom with the door closed and a pillow over her head, sound asleep. Flynn had reached the end of his tolerance for his wife's lack of action, feeling this baby would not survive. He scooped his totally soaked, smelly little baby, wrapped her in a blanket, grabbed the diaper bag, and frantically drove the short distance to his parents.

Too impatient to find the key on his keychain, he banged on the front door. His parent's response was immediate; Etta bolted from her room, followed by Owen from his. The door flung open, and Flynn, without hesitation, passed the baby to his father's arms.

Completely oblivious to Flynn's actions, Monique slept well past nine. After listening for the baby, she got up and brewed herself a glorious pot of coffee, almost as if she was in a dream of being in some serene, far away land. Despite the total calamity of the living room, she lingered in the indulgence of the delicious brew. Slowly, as she began to return to her reality, she became aware she was alone and was grateful for the solitude.

By this time, Lily's wellness was restored by her loving, nurturing, adoring grandparents. Sensing the calmness, Flynn retreated to his bed in his parent's home.

Monique went back to bed for a while. Later, she had a long, soothing bath with Epsom salts and washed her hair. After lunch, she painted her nails red while listening to Perry Como and Dean Martin on the radio. Later in the afternoon, a reminder of reality crept back while staring at the total upheaval of the apartment. She strolled into the baby's room, wrinkled her nose at the mess and smell, then closed the door, leaving the soiled baby bedding behind.

Owen came to the apartment door with a basket of egg salad sandwiches, lemonade, and Queen Elizabeth cake for Monique. He saw what he needed to reassure himself that she was ok and chalked the whole episode up to the fragility of women following childbirth.

Etta was busy oscillating between the delight of looking after her precious granddaughter and disdain of her predictably disgraceful daughter-in-law's behaviour. *What did Son expect marrying a pea wobbler?* Fatigue quickly became the common denominator for the caregivers, while baby Lily thrived in all the love and tender care of her grandparents.

Flynn was cautious around Monique, giving her time and space. He had two days off and wanted to review their course of parenting. Flynn decided to do what Monique liked to do. He took her for a car ride north to Pancake Bay for the afternoon to have a picnic on the beach. The wind was brisk, but the sun was shining, and he could see Monique's radiant smile return. That afternoon their playful beach blanket exchanges reassured Flynn that some familiarity of why he married Monique remained. On the return ride home, Monique's smile faded, as did her happy demeanour.

While they were out, Owen brought groceries to their apartment and once again transformed the chaos into shining order.

Owen decided it was time to reunite his son's little family. Etta resigned to the idea, given the sleepless nights she and Owen had suffered. Shortly after Monique and Flynn returned to the apartment, Owen arrived with the sleeping babe in his arms, passing her to Monique. Awkwardly, she took the baby, trying to find a comfortable holding position for herself. Owen didn't stay but gave his son an encouraging nod to signal that it was his time to man up beyond survival mode and get his family on a sure and steady course.

As Flynn closed the door behind his father, he felt disoriented with little confidence in righting the course.

Monique quickly passed Lily to Flynn while she retreated to the kitchen to sterilize the baby bottles. Her natural default to managing her new role of motherhood was to approach it from a clinical level. Eight bottles were perfectly prepared, six for the next twenty-four hours, plus two for the lead time into the following day until the process required repeating.

Despite getting the knack of changing diapers, Monique detested feeding time. She propped her baby on her side with a diaper rolled up and tucked tightly against her tiny back. Another diaper was rolled up, positioning the bottle so Lily could suck its contents without being held.

After a week of day shifts, Flynn had two weeks of graveyard shifts. This was when the mothering and infant care necessity fell apart. After Flynn's first shift of nights, when he returned to their apartment at 7:30 a.m., he hoped to have Monique smiling with babe in arms, both smelling fresh and oozing contentment. Breakfast would've been a bonus (but not necessary). His hope was not the reality of what he encountered. Flynn opened the bedroom door; Monique once again was sound asleep with a pillow over her head. He went to the unsettlingly quiet baby's room. Relief cast over him as Flynn saw Lily's chest expanding and her tiny body squirm under a blanket in the disheveled bassinet. He picked up his soaked baby girl and kissed her gently on top of her head to not scratch her with his overnight whisker growth. Flynn uselessly called out for Monique, but there was no response. Once again, but with more intent, he called. Overwhelmed, he wrapped up his daughter and drove to Simpson Avenue.

Etta predicted her son's arrival time and had a toasted tomato and bacon sandwich waiting for him. Flynn could smell the familiar heartwarming aroma of bacon; he drew a strained smile and passed the baby to his mother.

Etta and Owen had purchased a full set of all the baby needs which filled their transformed dining room. Etta had the baby bathtub, fresh baby clothes, and a bassinet already set up, anticipating her son's requirement for ongoing support. Already, Lily had a significant diaper rash due to lack of frequent diaper changing.

The new regime evolved to Monique only seeing Lily for the lunchtime feeding. Monique would have the next round of sterilized baby bottles, each filled with the exact amount of formula. Then Owen would take the baby back to Etta until the next day. Baby Lily and mother were perfectly content with that schedule.

On Flynn's days off, he and Monique would take the drive along Lake Superior and, on some occasions, stay overnight in Wawa. Monique and Flynn re-established their hot and steamy escapades, and both reaffirmed their love for one another. By mid-October, Monique was pregnant again.

As Flynn would say, "All hell broke loose!" It was a busy winter with the move to a small wartime house on the Township Line, bought at the significantly reduced rate for a veteran of WWII of twenty dollars a month mortgage. (Many of the months, Flynn would have to ask his parents for the money.) The downside was that it was five miles from Simpson Avenue. Monique was pleased to be further away from Etta's scorn.

Adele and Jacque saw their granddaughter for the first time at Christmas dinner at the farm. Adele grinned at the baby and returned to ricing her boiled potatoes while Jacque took his granddaughter and held her dearly in his arms, kissing the top of her little head. He took her out of the chaos of the country kitchen into the quiet living room with Flynn, offering him some of his homemade wine.

Soon enough, the peaceful holiday mood was transformed by a hostile mother and daughter shouting match. "I tried to warn you, Monique. Those damn Protestants will never accept your Catholicism. To them, you're nothing more than a DP."

Monique knew her mother was right but wouldn't concede. "They will want Lily to be Anglican, you know!" (Monique hated Etta for secretly having Lily baptized at St. Luke's two months prior.)

Despite the heated discussion—although Monique was still fuming—the turkey came out of the wood-burning oven as delectable as ever. All the traditional French side dishes were placed on the family table, including the much-anticipated tourtiere and the butter tarts.

When Adele finally sat down, she bowed her head, as did the rest, and said, "For all of the Catholics here, let us pray."

Before she could utter the next few words of grace, Monique had flung a big heap of riced potatoes, hitting her mother squarely on the forehead. The family fell silent, all glaring at Monique.

"Flynn, let's go. Now!" Readily, Flynn scooped the baby up while Monique took the butter tarts.

Flynn's relief was two-fold: to have escaped that feud and also to be on his way to his mother's Christmas turkey and plum pudding rum sauce.

Monique sobbed the whole way, getting Lily's white baby bonnet wet with snotty tears.

CHAPTER 13
MONIQUE PREGNANT AGAIN

As January rolled around, Monique finally revealed to Flynn that she was pregnant again. Monique had to admit to herself the "Rhythm Method" was not working for this highly-charged sexual pair. Monique would forget to take her morning vaginal temperature, let alone chart it over the month. Intimacy, for them, was the only true way they could right the chaos of their lives. Intensity and density were necessary for both of them, and they found it in their profoundly passionate, organic lovemaking.

Monique felt total freedom in the arms of her husband. She loved having his whole body covering and protecting hers. She wanted to remain hidden from all the judgements and persecutions beyond their bedroom walls.

For Flynn, he wanted and needed to arouse his beautiful wife. He loved to see her bloom over and over again.

Winter turned to spring, and soon it was the end of June and time for the first haying. Jacque made the call to Monique; they hadn't spoken since that unholy Christmas dinner fiasco. They managed a brief exchange of niceties, where Monique conveyed she was once again pregnant. He didn't react to the news and simply told her he needed Flynn to help with the haying. As the summer progressed, Monique remembered how much she hated being pregnant.

It was too hard to lift the now fourteen-month-old Lily, who refused to learn to walk. She told Flynn—in no uncertain terms—that his parents had spoiled their daughter. Lily was proudly carried everywhere or wheeled up and down Simpson Avenue for the neighbours to admire the privileged baby beauty.

One afternoon while Owen was out with Lily, Etta saw a cute white polar bear on four wheels in the new edition of the Eaton's catalogue. It was a walker designed for babies advancing to toddlers. (Etta was also silently concerned that Lily had no desire to attempt walking.) Privately, she would scold Owen for "carrying that baby too much." Etta didn't want to hear her next door neighbor, Edith, to utter one more time, "My granddaughter started walking at twelve months old."

During the last couple of weeks of the pregnancy, Monique didn't see Lily at all. This was of no mind to Lily, as she knew her grandparents to be her loving parents, and Monique and Flynn were visitors to her little-indulged world of affectionate nurturing.

With the last trimester of Monique's second pregnancy, their marital lovemaking had to be adjusted. Flynn loved to kiss the back of his wife's neck while slowly caressing her. It didn't take long with the altered posturing to excite all of their erogenous zones. After their usual intense passion simultaneously concluded, they collapsed to their side of the bed, oblivious to the burst of sanguineous fluid in the middle of their love nest.

It was a few hours before Monique awoke with intense pelvic pain combined with a tightening abdomen. Flynn reached over through his sleepy muse to be suddenly awakened by his wife's organic moaning.

"Ok, I've got this. Hold tight."

Despite this being their second child coming, they were even less prepared than the first. Flynn pulled on his pants, grabbed his soiled tee-shirt from the prior day's haying, and covered Monique in the bedspread that was beside his farming clothes on the floor. Getting Monique in the car and racing down Highway Seventeen to downtown, he wisely remembered to never bring his wife to the Plummer Hospital again. At General Hospital's emergency entrance, Flynn laid on the horn. Two hospital orderlies in their white uniforms quickly maneuvered Monique out of the car and into the wheelchair already in motion toward the delivery room.

Taking a deep breath, Flynn didn't proceed to the parking lot but turned the car back on Queen Street toward Simpson Avenue. Exhausted, he went around to the back door where Etta was already waiting with a look of concern and relief that her son was home.

It was two in the morning. Flynn did what all sons do in their mother's kitchen, he opened the fridge door and reached for the left-over chicken and a beer. Etta buttered the bread and layered the chicken generously in between the slices. *Ahh.* Those finer moments of unadulterated motherly attention rushed over him like a warm sea breeze. Food and ale tempered Flynn's anxiety, and he headed toward his boyhood bedroom. Etta and Owen acknowledged to each other with a glance about their son's foul odour and disheveled condition.

Owen arose, delighted to meet the new day with his Lily. Etta met them in the kitchen while Owen placed Lily in her highchair to play with her toy doll. Etta made cream of wheat while Owen warmed Lily's bottle.

Etta, realizing her son was still sleeping, rushed upstairs (knowing that he would sleep through her downstairs calling to him). "Son, wake up. You need to get to the hospital."

The word "hospital" stung his brain, and he jumped out of bed.

Etta had already laid out some fresh clothes. A few minutes later, she had a plate of bacon and eggs ready for him to hoover down with freshly percolated coffee. Once in the car, Flynn was deeply relieved his mother didn't ask him what hospital Monique was in.

CHAPTER 14
BABY NUMBER TWO

On arrival to the maternity ward, the head nurse greeted Flynn with a scowl. "Where have you been? We've been trying to reach you. Monique had a difficult delivery, and your baby girl has defects."

All he heard was "defects" and collapsed to his knees as if both Achilles tendons had been slashed. Huge tears immediately flowed down his unshaven face.

Two nurses helped Flynn to his feet. "We had to sedate Monique early on in the delivery. She doesn't know about the baby yet. We had to get the baby out with forceps, and Monique tore badly in the process."

Flynn only heard some of the words but made no sense of any of the information. The nurses led him to the nursery, where he saw a beautiful bundle of blonde-haired, sleeping joy. He only saw peaceful perfection until the doctor beckoned him to come into the nursery. Once gowned, a nurse handed Flynn his baby girl.

The infant naturally snuggled into his soothing hold. After a moment of greeting, the doctor took the baby to the examining table and unwrapped the swaddled baby, exposing her perfect little hands and hugely deformed feet. "Your baby has club feet. This is the worst case I've ever seen. It does not happen often; medical belief is that it's caused by extreme uterine pressure."

Flynn's mind immediately went to their tumultuous lovemaking with intense thrusting each time. Already grief-stricken, he heard the doctor say he had made a referral to Sick Kids Hospital in Toronto for an orthopaedic surgeon to assess and likely amputate both feet.

"These matters need to be dealt with quickly to lessen the burden caused by delaying the inevitable," the doctor firmly stated. The baby was rewrapped and peacefully placed back in the bassinet.

It was nine in the morning, and Monique was having her breakfast in bed. Monique recalled that this was the best part of delivering a baby; the small creature comforts following labour.

Because their baby was born with a deformity, the head nurse decided it was best not to upset the other mothers, so Monique was given a private room.

Flynn cautiously entered her room. "Hi," he said quietly. Monique was more interested in her warm toast with strawberry jam. "How are you feeling? I know this wasn't easy for you."

Monique continued casually sipping her tea. Nursing school taught her she needed to rebuild her strength, and she had a whole ten days to do it. She finally noticed the thick padding between her legs and the ooze accumulating behind her sacrum. Still numb from the Demerol, Monique didn't realize the extent of her vaginal tearing or that she had delivered anything but a perfect baby, hopefully a boy.

Flynn sat down in the chair beside her and rubbed her legs gently as he pressed his forehead into the bed so Monique wouldn't see his grievous face.

Monique dozed off to the rhythm of his hands moving up and down her legs. All she needed was her husband's attentive touch to feel her world was protected again.

Around eleven in the morning, the doctor entered the room with the head nurse, who was holding the baby. "Flynn, I'm sure you've informed Monique by now. Your appointment at Sick Kids in Toronto is scheduled for two weeks from today. I expect Monique will be away with your baby girl for a month. Please make your plans accordingly." With that, he left the room while the head nurse placed the baby in Monique's arms.

Monique's absent gaze reaffirmed that she was still drugged and had no idea of what was going on. All she said was, "Is lunch here yet?"

Flynn failed miserably at trying to stifle his anguish as he took the baby from his otherwise occupied and heavily medicated wife. His heart swelled with immense love and devotion when he was holding his new baby girl, just like he'd felt holding Lily for the first time. However, this time, all those feelings were mixed with panic; he had absolutely no idea how to navigate the impending doom of her deformities.

Monique didn't regain her faculties until the next day and was alert when the nurse wheeled the baby in for her morning bottle feed. "Good morning, Sunshine. Here's your baby girl."

Another girl. Oh well, no boy for Flynn, she thought while taking the babe and the warm bottle from the nurse. Somewhat ashamed, she realized she hadn't asked anything about the baby yet, but all she saw was another little angel. This baby was so blonde compared to Lily, who was dark-haired. Monique continued her investigation to typically count all fingers and toes.

A blood-curdling moaning escalated to a grievous trembling in her core. She screamed internally, *My mother was right! God has marred my baby!* Monique was inconsolably wailing. "My baby is deformed. My baby is deformed."

The maternity ward immediately went into lockdown. All the doors to the patients' rooms were closed tight. No one was allowed on the floor except the summoned doctor, who quickly filled a syringe with Haldol. Two large orderlies assisted the doctor in rolling Monique onto her side, exposing her buttock.

The doctor administered the injection and gently rolled her back while the nurse quietly tried to reassure Monique that it would be ok, and she should rest. Monique took heed to the rest suggestion and sunk into a paralytic repose.

"Did no one prepare Monique before she saw the baby's feet? Did her husband not tell her?" The doctor asked in a reprehensible voice.

Vacant looks back to the doctor was all the information he required. His look lightened as he said, "This would be hard for anyone to bear; no one is to blame here." As he said these words, he knew if anyone was to be incriminated, it should rest upon himself. He remembered Monique from her nursing career and knew under her stiffly starched uniform was a fragile woman. "Call her husband and ask him not to come in today. I don't want anyone to disturb her." The doctor left the room without another word.

Dutifully, the nurse called Flynn at his mother's number. "Monique has had a bad reaction to seeing the baby's deformities. The doctor has medicated her and asked that no one disturb her. Please do not come in until tomorrow."

Flynn could feel his chest and throat tighten as he responded, "Ok" and hung up the phone.

Etta could see something dreadful was happening. "Is the baby ok? Is Monique dying?" Silently and without remorse, she hoped for the latter.

Flynn sensed he had to man-up for this ordeal, but he couldn't muster any innate strength to face this catastrophe. He bent over and unashamedly cried in absolute despair.

Etta shuttered with fear as she called Owen at work, stressing he come home at once.

Owen had never had a call from home at work before. Without hesitation, he proceeded homeward. The beauty of the day did not reflect the impending storm.

When Etta met him in the doorway, her look of despair confirmed something horrible had happened to his family.

Baby Lily was crying in her crib. Neither Flynn nor Etta had the wherewithal to pick her up and reassure her that all was well. Owen quickly responded by priority. First, Lily was retrieved in his arms, artificially mustering a smile and hello to his precious granddaughter. Next, he sought out Flynn in his room, where he found his son facedown on the bed. "Son, tell me what's wrong. Your mother is frantic. I sent her for a nap".

After a long pause, Flynn raised his head, rolled to sit up, and looked his dad in the eyes. "Dad, our baby is deformed. She has a severe case of club feet, and the doctor is recommending amputations. Monique isn't handling it well; they have shot her full of sedatives. Dad, I don't know what to do." Flynn's desperation was apparent on his face and in his shaky voice.

Still holding Lily close to his chest, Owen said with calm resolve, "Son, this is terrible news. I can't believe it either. Whatever happens, your mother and I are here for you no matter what."

Flynn wholeheartedly believed his father; however, the pain in his chest wasn't relieved. Still sitting on the side of the bed, Flynn bent over and buried his face in his hands to try and conceal the tears.

Owen sat beside him and, with his free arm, reached around to hug his son.

CHAPTER 15
MONIQUE AND PSYCHIATRY

Monique awoke the following morning to discover she wasn't in a regular hospital bed but a standard twin bed in a light pink-colored room. She noticed the lack of antiseptic smell, and then it hit her: she must be in the psychiatric ward. Sure enough, when the nurse brought in her breakfast, she confirmed Monique's assumption. The nurse relayed that Monique suffered a "nervous breakdown" and needed to stay in the psychiatric ward for awhile. The nurse left out the part where Monique was an utter disturbance to the otherwise happy place of the maternity ward. Even the baby was moved to the dark hallway outside the nursery, away from the "perfectly normal" babies. Rumours were already spreading, and Monique's newborn was being referred to as "that deformed baby, the one that has to have her legs cut off."

Five days following Monique's delivery, she still hadn't seen her baby or her husband. Monique felt sheltered in her pink room. The medication kept coming, and she was relieved to have its numbing effect.

Eventually, the doctor wanted to cut back on the medication. "Monique needs to get prepared to deal with her baby's birth defects. Her appointment with the Toronto Orthopaedic Surgeon is in one week. Monique needs to take her baby there."

The nurse informed Monique of the doctor's plan when she delivered her morning breakfast tray without the accompanying pills. "I'll call your husband to come in today after his shift. In the meantime, the orderly will take you to the nursery to see your baby," she said. Monique didn't want to face either.

Monique chose the wheelchair ride as opposed to walking to see her baby. She started to feel anxious; she felt sweaty, and her body was tensing up.

A nurse had a quiet back corner ready for Monique with a cushioned rocking chair. The orderly helped her stand and assisted her to the chair. A few minutes later, the nurse returned with her swaddled baby and a warm bottle of formula. This was the second time she held her second child. The baby smelled so good; she made soft cooing noises that would melt any mother's heart—except Monique's.

Monique, besieged with fear, quietly said, "Please don't let this be. God, please don't punish me for all of my sins. Dear God, please." Monique tried to hold it together; her baby needed her. This wasn't going to be easy. "Mom was right; God didn't forget my mortal sin. I was foolish to believe all was forgiven when Lily was born. I was such a fool to think purgatory was going to be bypassed."

The baby started crying because the chair wasn't rocking and was unsupported in Monique's awkward hold. The nurse approached Monique as she tried to get a grip on her racing anxieties and hovered over the mother and child. After the twenty minutes were up, Monique asked to go back to her room.

Monique was regimented to receive sleeping medication only at night; the doctor was adamant that she be alert and dealing with her circumstance. Three times a day, she was wheeled to the baby, a necessary regiment to prepare Monique to travel with her baby to Toronto.

The doctor met with Flynn a few days later and explained everything was set up in Toronto for the baby's admittance to the Sick Children's Hospital. Monique could stay in the hospital until the day of departure to Toronto.

Before the doctor left, he said to Flynn, "By the way, what's this baby's name? We've only been using the last name. I need this information for the admission documents. You have until tomorrow, ok?"

Later that day, around the supper table at Etta and Owen's house, Lily was in her highchair, squishing her green peas with her spoon, waiting for her ice cream. While Etta was in the kitchen, Flynn said to Owen, "Dad, Monique and the baby are taking the train to the Toronto hospital on Monday. I need to give the hospital the baby's name by tomorrow." Monique hadn't said a word about her choice for a girl's name. "We were convinced we were having a boy this time, so I don't have any idea what it should be. I have to do it, though."

Owen drew in on his Export A, pondering the issue. "How about Nia, meaning bright, as in lustre, like the brightest star in the sky. It is a beautiful Welsh name; your mother loves that name. If you had a sister, that would've been her name."

"I like it. Nia will be her name," said Flynn, and they went to the kitchen to pour a jigger of rum for each of them.

Etta had figured out that Monique was not at the Plummer hospital; however, she certainly didn't anticipate her to be in a psych ward. (Knowing this, she was relieved Monique was not at the Plummer hospital where her friends would get wind of her now crazy daughter-in-law.)

Flynn hadn't returned to their house on the township line for over two weeks. Owen had correctly predicted the door was left unlocked for the duration of Monique's hospitalization. The place was in shambles. His task was to pack a suitcase for Monique to go to Toronto. It was Labour Day weekend, still warm. He did his best to find a nightgown, a sweater, a skirt, and a pair of pants. Everything he picked out needed to be washed and ironed. Owen was grateful he didn't bring Etta along; she would only have more ammunition to hate their daughter-in-law. Flynn went fishing with his buddies. Owen felt that was a good thing; his son needed a break from his sad situation. He set to work in the kitchen and ended in the bathroom. When everything was in order and shiny, he scooped up the soiled clothes and drove home, enjoying long drags on his Export A.

Etta had supper ready for her husband's return, and Lily sat in her highchair, delighted with her mashed potatoes and a big lump of butter melting on the top. "Owen, you look exhausted. What took you so long?" she asked. "I made pork chops for you with chopped cabbage and your favourite cucumber salad." That sounded like music to Owen's ears.

The following morning, Owen handed his son the suitcase of impeccably cleaned, folded, and packed clothing for Monique plus an envelope with $100 dollars in it. "Son, give this to Monique; I want her to have some spending money."

Flynn was grateful as he took the case and the cash. They nodded, and off Flynn went to pick up his wife and new his baby girl. He made a quick stop at the corner store to buy a chocolate cherry blossom before going to the hospital. He knew this would put a smile on his wife's face.

With the baby in her arms, Monique was already at the front door of the hospital waiting for him. She looked so pretty standing there despite the ordeal they'd been through. While getting ready, Monique found her red lipstick in her purse, and as per usual, she applied the lip colour. Once again, she could see and feel her face transform to her seemingly confident, beautiful self with a knockout smile. Monique was happy to be finally leaving the hospital. The breakfast in bed routine was getting old, as was the already memorized, repeating menus. She wouldn't miss the Wednesday night stew with the over-cooked, tasteless peas.

Flynn mustered a smile from somewhere deep within himself. He exited the car to greet his wife with a kiss on her cheek before helping her and the baby into the vehicle.

Still holding the baby, Monique eased into the familiar passenger seat. She was grateful to have a brief feeling of normalcy in the comfort of their car. Flynn extended his arm to reach over her shoulders and hugged her as he drove to the train station.

When they arrived, it was already time to board the train. On the platform, Flynn kissed Monique, then kissed the top of his baby's head and said, "Be brave, my little Nia."

That was the first time Monique had heard her daughter's name. It didn't distress her that she didn't have any input into the choice of her baby's name. The soft and loving sound of Flynn's voice saying "my little Nia" was all she needed to know about the choice of her second daughter's name.

Flynn remembered to pull from his pocket the envelope from his dad and the cherry blossom chocolate treat. Monique was delighted with both. As they got to the steps of the train, he hugged her one more time. Monique was ready to hear his declaration of "I love you." Instead, he emphatically stated, "No amputations."

CHAPTER 16
MONIQUE IN TORONTO

Monique always loved the passenger train, and this ride was even more special because she had a sleeper cabin. One hour into the trip, the steward came by with beverages, and she ordered a rum and Coke. "Ahhh," she murmured as the liquid went down so neatly. Her thoughts went to Flynn and how she already missed him. She thought of Lily briefly, about how beautiful she was. She also felt relieved that her short stay in the psych ward afforded her time to be out of the fray of the "deformity" upheaval. Monique started thinking about this horrid "Act of God" but quickly redirected her focus back to her delightful libation.

Like her mother, baby Nia loved the motion of the train and slept peacefully in the cabin's baby hammock. The Catholic Women's League was notified of Monique's situation while she was in the hospital and how she had to travel with a newborn to Sick Kids Hospital. They gifted a beautiful travel bag of rose-scented hand cream, practical postpartum white underpants and pads, and a long, pink nightgown with matching slippers. For the baby, they provided some hand-knit booties. Monique immediately knew her daughter's little hairpin turned ankles and feet would regrettably never don them. However, she was certain her bright little star would wear the matching sweater and bonnet, delicately interwoven with white ribbons.

When the steward came by again, Monique asked if he could warm the baby's bottle and bring her another cocktail. A short while later, dinner arrived. Monique was hungry and welcomed the roast beef with gravy, boiled potatoes, and green beans, followed by a slice of warm apple pie. A few hours later, as she savoured the cherry blossom Flynn had given her, she realized she hadn't felt this degree of well-being for a very long time. The rumble of the train rocked mother and baby fast asleep.

Monique awoke suddenly with the steward shouting in the hallway. "Toronto, Union Station. Toronto, Union Station." Monique took her time getting herself and the baby ready. She knew it would be a short taxi ride to the hospital.

As she stepped off the train with her baby, the porter was ready to load her luggage onto his dolly to assist her to the taxi area on Front Street. Inside the lobby, Monique allowed herself a lingering moment to absorb the grandeur of the Royal York Hotel across from the train station. She'd been there a few times with her nursing girlfriends for some wild weekends of sipping gin martinis in the Library Lounge. *Ah, the attention they did attract!*

Monique's mood remained upbeat while she took her time in the station's ladies' room to put on the skirt with the new long sheer stockings Owen had packed for her. Like always, she made sure the seams were perfectly centred down the back of her sleek, long legs. Her signature red lipstick always magically elevated her demeanour. Nia slept nearby while her mother allowed herself some brief moments of indulgence.

The children's hospital was awaiting the arrival of that Northern Ontario baby girl who possibly had the worst case of club feet the hospital had ever seen. Monique took a deep breath of relief when the admitting nurse put her baby in what looked like an elevated oversized metal cage on wheels. It hadn't been a full twenty-four hours yet, and she appreciated the brief sense of freedom.

The attending orthopaedic surgeon asked two of his colleagues to join him during the assessment and decision process to evaluate their limited treatment options. The evaluation would take until Thursday. *Wow, two whole days in Toronto to be fancy-free*, she thought to herself.

Monique, being a registered nurse herself, was welcomed at the nursing residence on Gerard Street. As a professional courtesy, the downtown hospitals always kept a room for visiting nurses requiring accommodation. This was just what she needed and wanted; the city life in the final days of summer with her carefree capsule of time, her red lipstick, and the envelope inside her purse with the one-hundred dollars.

Her first luxury was to go to the movies to see "Sabrina" with Audrey Hepburn (who she secretly likened to herself) and Humphrey Bogart. Delighted to be seeing this movie, she splurged on a cherry Coke and some buttered popcorn. Monique lost herself in the mesmerizing romantic comedy. Later that evening, it wasn't hard for her to fall asleep in the crisp, white sheets made up with perfect nurses' corners.

Monique spent the following day shopping. Simpson's Department Store had their new line of fall fashions displayed in the storefront windows, beckoning her in; Eaton's Department Store had the same effect on this pretend movie starlet. By the end of the day, she'd purchased a new red car coat, black leather gloves, and the perfect red chiffon turban to emulate the Hepburn look. Flynn would surely say, "Monique, you're a knockout!"

Monique returned to the residence for a light dinner and rest. She had plans for the evening and had no aversion to being unescorted; in fact, she preferred it that way. Living a little on the edge was easily retrieved from her previous life escapades. She took the streetcar to the Royal York Hotel and did what every drop-dead gorgeous woman does; she allowed the doorman to open the door for her to make her movie star entrance. Monique continued her solo parade to the Library

Lounge. It was a Wednesday night and, just as she predicted, full of suited-up businessmen.

Before she was even settled in her seat at the bar, a man was at her side, assisting her out of her coat. "What's the lady drinking tonight?" he said as if he was from a Humphrey Bogart movie.

She replied in a confident low voice, "Gin Martini, straight up with a twist ."

"Cigarette?" the gentleman asked.

Flawlessly she inhaled, as she had seen many times in the movies. There was little conversation between the two at the bar. Both were enjoying the ambiance, the allure of the moment, and the alcohol. Upon finishing her drink, she nodded to the gentleman with a "Thanks for the drink" and sashayed to the powder room. Ahhh, it was exactly how she remembered the loo to be with its huge, gold framed mirror. Her reflection was truly beaming as she touched up her classic red lips. After blotting her lips on a tissue, she returned to her testosterone-loaded audience.

Another gentleman was waiting for her to return to the lounge. He confidently took her hand, leading her to his table. With her seductive nod, the gentleman lifted his hand with two fingers. The bartender repeated Monique's drink as she knew he would. Again, there were a limited amount of niceties. After the drink, Monique arose; this time, she headed for the front door motioning to the doorman to summon her a cab. It had been a perfect evening of affirming her readily-retrievable, seductive self. She needed that escapade of an evening to balance what she knew she had to face the next morning.

The following morning, she arrived promptly at nine for the meeting with the surgical team. In preparation, she put on her clinical nurse persona. To survive this necessity, it was the only way she knew how to be strong enough. The head surgeon started by saying, "Your doctor in the Sault was right when he referred your daughter here. This is a very severe case of Congenital Talipes Equinovarus, otherwise known as club feet. I haven't seen a case so severe." He paused for a moment before proceeding. "I've consulted with my colleagues here as well as a New York paediatric orthopaedic surgeon, and our treatment options are very limited." The word "limited" felt like a bullet in the gut. The surgeon continued, "If we do nothing, your child will likely never walk, given that her feet are turned in so badly that she would be walking on the outside of her ankle bones. We see this in third world countries, and the quality of life for these kids is painfully grim in all aspects. We could try multiple surgeries followed by multiple long-term serial casting, trying to elongate the already underdeveloped group of tendons and muscles. Quite likely, we'll arrive at the same place of non-function, not to mention an extremely painful pair of little feet. The other option is to quickly and efficiently deal with this matter with amputations."

Monique heard that unavoidable word again—amputations—and knew that Flynn would absolutely not accept cutting off his daughter's feet. In her very clinical stature and voice, she stated, "There will be no amputations. We opt for the surgeries and casting. Yes, we realize there are no guarantees."

"Ok, Mrs. Kross, we'll proceed with the surgical and casting option," the doctor replied and left.

Monique's brief façade of strength melted in a puddle as she rushed to leave the hospital, not even stopping by to see her baby.

She returned to the nurses' residence, headed straight for her dorm room, and cried. She was deeply facing the truth she'd tried for days to avoid and cried deeper into the pillow to muffle her overwhelming sorrow. Monique watched the clock and waited until four p.m. when she knew Flynn would be finished his day shift and be back at his mother's place. She dialled the number, and Etta answered the phone. Monique could hear Lily giggling in the background. "Hello, is Flynn there?"

Etta instantly shouted, "Son, telephone."

Flynn was expecting this call. "Monique," he said into the receiver.

"Yes," was all she said, followed by a long, painful silence. Finally, she blurted out, "I said no to the idea of amputations."

"Good," he said in his stoic voice. He then crumbled with the following question, "What's next?"

Monique retold the surgeon and parent conversation regarding the options. They fearfully tried to pull it together despite only being connected by the telephone.

"How long before the surgeries?" Flynn finally asked.

"I don't know," Monique helplessly replied. Both realized the conversation was over by their mutually stunned and numb feelings.

Monique returned to the hospital the next day, this time seeing her infant. The orthopaedic ward nurse handed her the baby and a bottle and pointed to the rocking chair.

The nurse watched the pair and noted that the baby was undoubtedly beautiful, but there was an absence of joy and only fear in the mother's acknowledgement.

Monique decided not to unwrap Nia's blanket. She wanted to allow herself and her baby a few uninterrupted moments of a peaceful attempt at mother and child bonding.

"The doctor will see you now," the nurse said after several minutes.

Monique, still holding her baby, walked down the hall to meet the doctor. She felt cold and clinical, like she did in her days as an OR nurse, not as a scared mother worried about the pending surgeries for her infant.

"Good morning," the doctor said in greeting. "I'm making plans for the surgeries. We'll need to get started while all the tissues are still supple. There's going to be a lot of preparation work, like X-rays, measurements, and acquiring some additional precision surgical instruments. I expect we can do the first surgery one foot at a time, starting in ten days. The baby will need to stay here for the next few months."

Monique understood all of the jargon. However, she didn't expect such a lengthy time frame.

"I suggest you go home and leave your baby with us," the doctor recommended.

Monique kissed Nia on the top of her head, left the hospital, and was on the afternoon train heading back home. While she didn't have enough money for a sleeper cabin, she did have a few dollars left for a couple of stiff rum and Cokes.

CHAPTER 17
HELLO LITTLE STRANGER

The train ride north was uneventful. Flynn had taken the day off to pick up Monique and go to their home to grieve this tragedy of a less than perfect baby together. They wanted to handle this situation in bed, holding each other tight and getting lost in their passionate lovemaking. The mood was not robust and sultry; it was melancholy. They stayed interlocked for quite some time, trying to have emotional comfort rather than orgasmic ecstasy, which was their norm.

A few days passed, and Owen arrived with Lily in tow. Flynn was at work when Monique's father-in-law opened the side screen door. He brought only a few of the toddler's favourite things, as Etta didn't want the other toys "ruined" by her daughter-in-law's lack of attention. Etta was angry with Owen's unilateral decision to return Lily to her parents for a few days. He said, "It's not right for a baby to be without her mother this long. We're wrong to keep her from her parents' care."

Etta knew he was right; however, intuitively, she knew Monique would never be able to meet the task, certainly not by her standards.

Owen didn't come in; he just passed Lily over to Monique, who said, "Hello, little stranger." *What an admission of detachment,* he thought and was thankful Etta didn't hear Monique's greeting.

Lily cried as her Papa left. When her crying turned into deep sobbing, Monique put Lily in her sterile room with a cold bottle of milk and shut the door. The afternoon didn't go well for either of them. Flynn returned home from his shift to find Monique and Lily both depleted from crying.

The little news they received from Toronto was not encouraging, and the days felt like weeks for all of them.

October arrived, and Nia had her first set of surgeries. Monique hadn't been back to Toronto for three weeks and was planning to go the following week. Flynn was working double shifts to get extra money to cover the added financial burden of having a sick child. It was cheaper if Monique went alone; he didn't have to miss work, and his hidden reprieve was that he did not have to deal directly with the hospital issues or see his baby suffer. For Monique, going to Toronto meant not being suffocated with trying to mother Lily.

This was taking its toll on the entire family. Lily became sullen and forlorn. She had no appetite, nor did she find interest in her structured day. If she wasn't in her crib, she was bundled up and put outside in the buggy "to get fresh air." Jigger, Flynn's trusty four-legged mate, was left in charge of protecting the area surrounding Lily. The highly-organized day was Monique's way of coping with what she felt were the overwhelming demands of mothering.

Lily still wasn't walking, nor did her parents playfully encourage her to ambulate. Owen dropped by periodically (Etta never wanted to go since she knew it would only upset her, and she didn't want to say anything to flare up Monique or her son), and he could see no one was thriving, least of all Lily. Again, he made the unilateral decision to scoop her up and return her to Etta's stabilizing and nurturing love and care.

Both Lily and Etta returned to their happy state within moments. Lily had her grandmother feeding her the food she loved, her favourite toys were in their places, and her bear with the walker frame was ready to roll.

Monique hadn't seen her parents since the previous Christmas with the potato heaving incident. One weekend when Jacque asked Flynn to help on the farm—despite it being his weekend off his day job—Monique went too. Deep down, she wanted to see her parents.

"Hi Mom," Monique casually said as she opened the door to the farm kitchen.

"Hi," her mother replied without emotion while rolling out a pie crust.

Monique reached for the kettle, filled it, and put it on the stove to make each of them a coffee. While the water was set to boil, Monique reached for two clean mugs from the dish rack. She placed them on the oilcloth-laid table where the spoons and instant coffee were placed. She then went to the fridge for the can of Carnation evaporated milk with the hole already punched in. The kitchen was uncomfortably silent aside from Adele's heavy-handed thudding of her rolling pin against the counter and the bubbling of the heating water. Both sat down, Adele in her usual spot and Monique in hers. "How's the baby, Monique? Your dad tells me she is in Toronto with deformed feet. Is this true?"

Monique quietly nodded in a sorrowful manner.

Adele took a long, undignified slurp of the hot coffee then reached for a pink wafer cookie that Monique had found in the pantry. She dunked the cookie in the coffee and leaned forward over the cup to catch the pink, coffee-soaked mush in her mouth. Adele finished the last swallow of her coffee. Monique knew this would be the moment of reckoning with her mother.

"Monique, I told you bad things would happen when you disobeyed me, God, and your father by marrying that Protestant. You are a very silly girl to believe otherwise!" So the rant went on and on.

While Flynn went to the field, Jacque hung back, not trusting Adele and Monique could be civil to each other. The gloves were definitely off. The words of mortal sin, commandments, obey, confession, bastards, purgatory, and hate flew like bullets from opposing sides. Monique was hysterical while Adele was escalating her hurtful pontificating.

"I hate you. I hate you," was all Monique could muster up in retaliation as Jacque entered the kitchen.

"Stop this now! Monique, get in your car and drive home," Jacque shouted.

Monique quickly left, knowing her father would drive Flynn home after getting a full day's work out of him.

Monique didn't remember the drive home. When she arrived, she sat in the driveway a long time, tormenting herself about her choices in life and fundamentally believing her mother's accusations and judgements. Eventually, she went into the house and packed for her Toronto trip, knowing that she would be miles away from her mother.

The next morning, Monique was tired and didn't feel up to packing Flynn a lunch before his seven-to-three day shift. Flynn opened a can of peaches, made some toast, and ate quietly in the small kitchen, knowing his wife was leaving for Toronto to see their suffering baby. How did his life get so upended? How did things get so beyond his control? He looked in his wallet, took out $150, and laid the money on their shabby kitchen table. That was all the money he managed to save. *Monique will have to make it last*, he thought to himself as he closed the door and headed off to work.

CHAPTER 18

BACK TO TORONTO

The sounds and the movement of the train to Toronto soothed Monique once again. Soon her thoughts drifted to a quiet splendour. Her tranquil mood ended when the conductor bellowed, "Union, Toronto Station."

Monique quickly turned her clinical mother role switch on and headed off to The Sick Children's Hospital. As she pulled the heavy front door open, the familiar hospital smell hit her olfactory nervous system, cueing her stoic clinical response to forge ahead.

Nia had been in the hospital's care for over a month. She was still in the orthopaedic ward at the end of the hall. All ten metal cribs in the sterile room had a tiny human form inside. Monique read the name cards at the end of each crib. In the far back corner was her baby. Nia was lying still on her back, her little hands clenched, and her eyes were staring blankly at the ceiling as if she was mesmerized by the cracks.

Monique's gut reaction to this sight was sickening. Her baby wasn't thriving. (What did she expect?) Monique pulled the small flannel sheet back and saw the heavy casting covering her scrawny little legs from the knees to the toes. Her baby couldn't move her legs as the casting was too weighted. Monique's nose scrunched from the foul smell coming from the diaper. Monique reached for one of the nearby sanitized diapers to replace the soiled one. Monique was shocked that the stench was evidence of diarrhea still oozing from Nia's raw, rash laden bottom. Her nurse training taught her that diarrhea in a baby this young could be fatal.

The nurse came into the room while Monique was still trying to manage the explosive situation. "Hello, Mrs. Kross. I wanted to give you a few minutes to get reacquainted with Nia."

"She is by no means doing well. Why didn't you let me know of her poor state?" Monique demanded.

"We knew you would be here today and decided not to alarm you and your husband unduly. I'm going to ask the doctor if we should start an IV today, as she isn't taking in any fluids," the nurse explained.

"This is very serious. I'm afraid she's going to die!" Monique responded frantically.

Monique quickly went into clinical action mode. She released the metal side rail; it descended, jarring Nia from her dulled state. Monique sensed her baby was too weak to cry, given her deteriorated condition.

The nurse explained a gastrointestinal bug started a week prior. "Nia has had diarrhea for the last four days. Her little bottom is raw because of the casting; we couldn't get the plaster wet, which prevented us from cleaning her properly."

Monique understood the rationale; however, she couldn't accept her baby withering away in runny excrement. The nurse informed her the casting had another month before the next round of surgery. Monique, summoning her clinical knowledge, could see her baby wouldn't survive another day with this degree of dehydration. Despite her flowing tears, Monique put into motion a gentle, thorough washing, avoiding the casting. She held the baby over the sink and let the warm water flow lightly and continuously over the raw, reddened areas. Nia responded to the gentleness and nurturing of her mother's touch. Monique saw the small baby bottles of sterilized water.

She grabbed her purse, knowing she had a few packets of sugar saved from the train in case there was no sugar at the residence. She then broke the bottle's seal, poured the contents of the sugar packet into the baby bottle, and shook it. Monique then warmed the bottle by running it under hot water. She took her weakened baby to the rocking chair in the hallway, realizing Nia needed her mother more than ever.

A few minutes later, Monique looked at her nursing watch, which she always wore. She knew the train schedule well. The north-returning train was one hour from departure time, which meant Monique had to make decisions quickly. With her baby in her arms, she hurried to the nursing station, the casted little legs clanked together the entire way. "I'm taking my baby home. She'll die if I leave her here." Monique paused to catch her breath. "I'll need some supplies."

The nurse behind the desk knew Monique was right but professionally said, "I will need to get the doctor's permission for discharge."

Monique didn't wait for the answer; she marched into the supply room as if she was the attending nurse and packed what she needed for the trip home. With the baby wrapped in hospital blankets, she proceeded to the elevator with the paper bag of supplies, her suitcase, and her purse. As she passed the desk, she said to the nurse, "Call my husband and tell him I am on my way home with our baby."

Outside the front door of the hospital, she luckily saw an available cab. "Train station, please, and hurry." Once in Union Station at the ticket booth, Monique was relieved there was a sleeping cabin available. *Thank God*, she thought to herself, grateful she had the money for this needed upgrade.

A porter quickly helped her get to the gate and moved her to the front of the pre-boarding line. Once in the confines of the sleeping cabin and the familiar soothing motion, Monique sighed and felt a huge sense of relief. She sat back, looking at her sleeping baby on the train cot, her bag of supplies, and her purse. Knowing she would have a long night of caring for the infant, she rang for the cabin steward and asked for a chicken salad sandwich, a butter tart, and a rum and Coke.

Despite the rocky night ride, both mother and baby were soothed. Every two hours, Monique woke her daughter to feed her the sweetened water. It was a small feat if the baby would drink at least one ounce. After the bottle, Monique gently washed the baby's raw bottom. Monique implemented a two-hour treatment regimen of hydration, cleaning, and airing of the rash, followed by sleeping throughout their trip home.

Flynn was waiting at the station as the train rolled in. He kept the car running, with the heater on, knowing the fall morning air would be too cold for the baby. He could see his wife descending the train stairs with the assistance of the conductor. Flynn's chest swelled with fear, love, devotion, and more fear. He held them both in his arms, and he tearfully said, "Let's go home."

CHAPTER 19
LILY, THE BIG SISTER

After a week of the strenuous regiment of restoring basic health to their infant, Flynn and Monique were anxious to have Lily finally meet her baby sister.

Etta reluctantly came with Owen to bring Lily back to her parents. Etta hadn't seen Nia yet (she would never step inside that dago hospital), and then her new granddaughter was whisked off to Toronto. In truth, she felt ashamed for her son to be living on the wrong side and outside of town.

The house was a small wood frame with two small windows at the front and a door with no steps (they couldn't afford them yet). Roof shingles for siding covered the exterior of the house. Mortified with the dwelling, Etta tried to avoid the puddles with her high heel shoes as she navigated toward the side door. Meanwhile, Lily was carefree and happy in her Papa's arms as he sang "Mary Had A Little Lamb" to her.

Inside, the tiny house was in shambles: dishes piled in the sink, dirty pots on the stove, the table still had egg streaked plates, and half-full cups of cold coffee were carelessly discarded around the kitchen.

Monique could see the predicted disdain of her mother-in-law but chose to be silent for Flynn's sake. She could not afford an emotional row now with Lily's homecoming and baby Nia napping in her crib in the second bedroom off the living room.

Monique lifted the heap of clean diapers off the couch that were just in from the clothesline, ready to be folded. She felt a running list of Etta's judgements like ticker tape as her eyes swept the room.

Etta could see the diapers were greyish and certainly not to her bleached standards. She'd prepared herself not to have even a cup of tea or have to need to use the bathroom—she knew it would be filthy. To ensure she would stay true to her strategy, she kept her ivory kid leather gloves on.

Flynn picked up Lily and took her to the bedroom, where Nia was just rousing from her morning nap. Monique stood by their side as Flynn said, "Lily, this is your new baby sister."

Not yet two, Lily tried to repeat the word sister, but it came out "Sissy."

Monique picked up Nia, quickly changed her, and then brought the fresh-smelling baby to her mother-in-law.

Etta momentarily softened toward Monique and her immense list of shortcomings and felt a warming joy cover her as she gazed at the blonde-haired, rousing, sweet-smelling baby working hard to open her hazel eyes. *Just like Flynn's*, she said to herself. Regardless of the weight of the discoloured plaster casts, Etta felt grateful; at that moment, there was an ever-so-brief feeling of all of them belonging together.

Lily cried as her Papa and Nana kissed her goodbye and sat her on the cold hardwood floor with her Raggedy Ann doll. Lily's crying frightened her Sissy, but neither Monique nor Flynn reached to reassure her; they were both caught up in their feelings of being overwhelmed once again. This was the first time all of their family was together.

A week passed, and no one was content except Nia. She was gaining some weight, her bottom was healing, and she savoured the rocking in her mother's arms. Lily became the child not thriving. She cried many times in the day until she discovered how to self soothe. She had a blanket in her crib with satin edging. She would rub the smooth fabric between her fingers on her left hand and then suck the index finger of her right hand. (This toddler obsession lasted well into her teenage years.) Lily's habit became so hardwired that even her Nana couldn't diminish or eliminate this need for Lily to comfort herself.

On the weekends, Lily would go to her grandparents to resume what Monique referred to as her daughter's "spoiled life." It was necessary to have a break from their restless, irritable, and discontented daughter. Flynn and Monique kept Nia with them.

Nia was much easier to satisfy; all she needed was to be held close and rocked. Monique liked this because she could relax with this child. For hours they would rock together, Monique singing softly all the Doris Day and Perry Como songs she knew. When Monique had had enough, she would put the lulled baby down in the crib, and she would go to her bed, and both would sleep for at least three hours. Flynn loved the weekends too; he enjoyed the quiet and the comfort of knowing at least two of his girls could be easily pleased.

Etta didn't want the responsibility of having Nia on the weekends. She was distressed with the casting because she felt it was evidence to her friends and neighbours that this grandchild was less than perfect.

Owen was relieved to have Lily back as he truly missed her. He didn't feel at ease for the whole week, worried that Flynn and Monique couldn't give Lily all the love and attention she needed.

On Sunday nights, Flynn, Monique, and Nia would come from the township for a beautiful family meal. On their arrival, Owen would have the makings of the usual cocktail hour before dinner. Monique and Flynn would have their rum and Coke on ice, Etta had her two jiggers of gin, and he would pour a whisky on the rocks for himself.

After five minutes of this appearance of togetherness, Etta would excuse herself and take her drink to the kitchen to "check on dinner." She loved having her son home for at least one meal a week. She could see he'd lost the carefree glint in his eyes. He was thin and tired looking (she knew this marriage would be the death of him).

The table was perfectly set, just like her mother had taught her. Her precious Rosebud pattern, Spode, would come out for its weekly display of English refinement. Flynn barely noticed the china, and Monique couldn't care less; they both were only interested in the roast beef and Yorkshire pudding. Owen was pleased to have Lily by his side at the dinner table, ensuring each spoonful was small enough for her to manage safely.

Like clockwork, Lily intuitively knew when it was time for her parents to take her back to the place that didn't feel like home. As her Papa butted out his after-dinner cigarette, Lily lunged for her blanket to rub the satin and already had her finger in her mouth, sucking fretfully. Both Etta and Owen had a sick feeling packing her up while kicking and screaming. This routine continued week after week.

It was a hard winter for all of them. They were snowed-in most nights. Flynn would set the alarm for 5:00 a.m. to start shovelling for at least an hour before returning to the warmth to make his breakfast. As he heated a can of whole tomatoes (familiar to him from his navy days called Red Lead) and made some toast, he would check to see if there was a lunch made for him. It was often a disappointment to see that his lunch pail was empty. The guys in the plant knew to bring extra for Flynn; they felt sorry for him having a deformed daughter.

Despite Lily's crying around 7:00 a.m., Monique wouldn't be roused to get up and make her children breakfast. Instead, she'd drift in and out of sleep for another hour or so. Lily would be screaming in her crib, saying, "Toast, toast, toast," as her little tummy was chewing on her backbone.

Monique hated the drudgery of the long Sault Ste Marie winters where sunshine was craved by this housewife stuck within the small frame of their wartime home. It was extremely hard for Monique to establish a nurturing rhythm for Lily. Each day they would be at odds with each other. For such a little being, she showed a lot of resentment toward her mother for not knowing how to please her. Monique would lament why Lily was so demanding, and Nia was so at ease and accepting without complaint regarding anything Monique had to offer.

Every other day was wash day. The never-ending pile of dirty diapers would be washed in the wringer washer, rinsed, and squeezed through the rollers to press out the water. Then they'd be placed in the basket to be hung outside. Monique would put on her ankle-high boots, her old winter coat with a kerchief tied around her head. She followed the little path Flynn would have shovelled in the morning, carrying the heavy load of wet diapers. As Monique climbed up onto the clothesline stoop, she'd plop the load down, bend over and pull one diaper out at a time, shake it out, and place the wooded clothes pins by the corners of the diaper. She'd repeat the process until thirty diapers were hanging, already stiffening in the frigid temperatures of the north. She tried to hurry this process as her long, delicate fingers would sting with the cold.

By the time Flynn returned from his shift, there would usually be a meal underway. Monique would have at least three pots on the stove boiling: one for potatoes, one for beans, and the other for carrots. Monique never got the timing, the amount of water, and the amount of heat just right. Usually, two out of the three pots had "scorched" vegetables; however, whatever the meat was, she always got that right. After the dinner (when he worked the day shift) during the week, Flynn would get ready to go out for either bowling or the rifle range for target practice.

Lily's second winter was met with distress each day. Her blanket was filthy and tattered, all but a few remnants of the satin edging remaining, her index finger bled every day, and her baby front teeth were starting to protrude from the frantic sucking. Still, the only one coping was Nia.

When April finally arrived, Lily took her first solo steps into her Papa's arms one week before her second birthday. It was Sunday evening. Flynn sat on the couch with Monique sipping on their cocktails while Lily had the expression of an Olympian crossing the finish line. Etta was in the kitchen with her roast beef and gin, and Monique was holding Nia, only mildly interested in her eldest daughter's achievement.

Lily lived in two worlds of feast or famine when it came to her attention-seeking. At a young age, she realized her world had polar opposites of well being. She felt neglect and abandonment from her parents and acted out at every opportunity. Her baby sister was treated differently.

Nia seemed numb to the chaos and seemed to have learned in her infancy that her crying couldn't be heard amongst the choir of wailing babies in the orthopaedic ward of the children's hospital.

Lily easily caught on to the cycle of once a month, Monique would pull out the brown suitcase. With this monthly pattern of activity, Lily would smile with excitement. She knew the next move would be to Simpson Avenue for the week, while her mother and little sister disappeared.

By the time Nia was one, the surgeries were completed. (Flynn was grateful he found the insight and the courage to hold strong to his decision of "no amputations.") By her second birthday (with rigid splinting and painful stretching exercises that Monique and Flynn performed daily), Nia learned to walk. Nia hated the Oxford boots she had to wear while growing up. She knew she was never going to be an athlete or ballerina. Despite the surgeries, her less than perfect little feet made it hard for her to keep up with the other kids. At least her feet were functional, and overall (in her world), Nia adapted to her foot issues as being her normal.

Regardless, Nia had traveled through a war zone. She felt immense abandonment, incredible fear, and the deepest of pain. Nia was caged (in an oversized hospital crib) for the first year of her life, like a helpless sick animal. With negligible human contact, hanging on to life (when she had contagious diarrhea), she naturally learned the psychological survival technique of numbing. Sad but true, Nia repressed these memories of her infant life. Her subconsciousness retained the learning about numbing, but when the pain became too great in her life, the effects of numbing resurfaced.

CHAPTER 20
NIA GROWING UP

Every day was a hard day for Lily and Nia. Monique was consistently absent, either in a sanitarium or doped up in her rocking chair, sleeping all day. The house was always disheveled, the refrigerator dependably empty, and their father was either at the plant trying to provide or retreating to find respite anywhere other than his address.

Technically, Lily and Nia weren't neglected, as their parents could be accounted for. Lily continued to evolve her rebel role, leaving Nia to be the reliable one. Every day, Lily would be irritable, and every day, Flynn would emotionally check out.

Payday was the only good eating day at their house. Monique, Lily, now ten, and Nia, now eight, would go to the grocery store after Flynn got home with the car. While Monique had her driver's license, it was debatable whether she should lawfully be allowed to drive. Reversing out of the driveway, it would take her several tries of grinding all of the gears to achieve the direction she wanted to go.

Flynn would watch the car proceed up Township Line toward Highway Seventeen. He shook his head in frustration when the brake lights stayed on despite the car being in third gear, headed for the intersection.

Lily rode shotgun, while Nia hung on to the armrest behind her mother to prevent sliding the other way when Monique was attempting to navigate. Once in the grocery store, the cart would quickly fill with the usuals. Nia looked forward to the treats like fresh, warm French bread and a jelly roll cake.

The girls' delight was predictably juxtaposed with humiliation as the cashier would ring up the total, and Monique would never have enough money. She would then pick the items to go back. Lily became used to the procedure; she had the strategy of getting the keys to the car ahead of the shameful checkout. On the other hand, Nia was expected to stay and help her mother select the items to be left behind. The trio would return home with a chuck steak to be fried, a green salad, some Spanish rice from a box, and jelly roll cake. The only other good eating day was Sunday dinner with their grandparents.

Lily grew tall and excessively lean. Nia was short and scrawny. Lily had the big beautiful brown eyes and long, satin, dark brunette hair and, despite her rebelliousness, was a true beauty. Nia never measured up to Lily's exquisiteness.

There was a steady, incremental increase in the level of discontentment in Nia's home; it was primarily based on religious issues and conflicts. It would start Saturday night after Lily and Nia would have a bath together. They had great delight in playing in the bubble bath and drawing basic images on each other's back while the other guessed what the drawing was. By the end of the bath time, *Hockey Night in Canada* would be on their black and white TV.

That was when Monique would demand everyone's shoes needed to be polished for Mass the next morning. The agony for all of the family predictably commenced. It would end with a very frustrated and angry father and a mother slamming the door to her bedroom. For Nia, a secure and nurturing household was unfortunately only recognizable in other peoples' homes.

Sunday morning, the row would continue. Flynn didn't want to go to Mass or any other church, for that matter. Despite all convincing efforts on Monique's part, she would drive herself and her children to Mass. As they entered the church, they dipped their fingers into the holy water and made the sign of the cross. Monique imagined all eyes were on her and her offspring without her husband attending. She felt judged and shamed for their obvious religious divide.

CHAPTER 21

NIA TAKES THE BUS

Nia was only nine when she felt she was ready (or not) to take her first solo ride on the city bus. The magnitude of this journey became evident as she stood on the side of the Trans Canada Highway Seventeen North. The cold, wet, and very windy March afternoon offered no comfort for the seemingly endless wait. The cars and transport trucks sped by, spraying the highway slush on her bare legs. The wind whipped her long, blonde, tangled, wet hair against her face. When the bus finally arrived, Nia could hardly see. She took the large steps up to face the burly bus driver. After dropping her hard-earned change into the coin box and heard its rattle to the bottom, she noted the impatient bus driver eyeing her up. He gave a quick nod, which meant she needed to get to her seat. He looked displeased about having to navigate back into the fray of transport trucks heading north.

The unoccupied seat Nia chose was frigid on her bare legs, and she could feel her wet skin sticking to the dirty, dark vinyl seat. Nia grabbed hold of the steel bar above the seat ahead of her, knowing she couldn't sit back and take any pleasure in the ride.

The bus proceeded way past the Davey Home for the Aged, opposite to where she wanted to go. Nia felt her apprehension rise as her singular plan to go downtown was going awry. A contingency plan didn't occur to her; it was all or nothing. Had she taken the wrong bus? Nia smirked and relaxed as she realized this was the only bus that came to the fringes of the steel town. Eventually, the bus signalled to turn around somewhere a few miles between the Fourth and Fifth line.

Nia could feel her shoulders descend a bit, as she felt reassured she was heading toward her southerly destination: downtown. Nia was excited yet felt somewhat guilt-ridden for deceiving her always-distracted mother. She told her mother she was just going to the "neighbours at the end of the road." Well, she certainly went to the end alright, and significantly beyond for her young, very inexperienced years of nine.

It was when she got to the top of Pim Hill that her heart stopped sprinting, as she knew she would soon be approaching the amazing Queen Street. The main street of this small Northern Ontario town seemed like New York's Park Avenue to Nia.

Her heartbeat went into overdrive again when she stepped off the bus in front of the only department store she knew, Kresge's. The place seemed massive and magical to her. The big glass doors at the entranceway pushed opened, and the washed-out, creaky, hardwood floor seemed marvellously glorious to the poor-heeled waif from the township. She had only been in this store a few times with her Nany and Lily. Similarly, she was mesmerized by all the merchandise as she strolled wide-eyed and bushy-tailed down each aisle.

Nia could smell the hamburgers frying and the shrilling sound of the machine preparing a chocolate milkshake in the frosted stainless-steel cup that she knew would soon to be poured into the tall funnelled glass with the well-positioned paper straw in the thick shake. Nia could hear the gastric juices flow in her empty stomach as she took in the aroma from the diner in that incredible department store. The reality was, though, that she had only seventy-five cents. If she wanted to buy herself something special and still afford the bus ticket home, she had no choice but to endure the pang of hunger.

She eventually navigated to the piece de resistance, the cosmetic aisle. Lingering over the lipsticks and the tantalizingly cheap eau de toilette, this vulnerable, pre-adolescent girl thought she was in Wonderland. Persian Lilac was Nia's favourite scent. She opened the small bottle and savoured the sweet fragrance, even though she knew she couldn't afford that decadence. Nia knew she couldn't bring home a lipstick, either, because the department store only had bright red ones like her mother wore. It would be much too conspicuous and improper for a nine-year-old to wear.

Nia vividly remembered how her mother would stroke her exquisite French-Canadian cheekbones with the stunning red lipstick and then blend it in with her fingertips. (Her mother used her lipstick for her lips as well as her cheeks since she couldn't afford rouge.) Nia also loved to watch her mother powder her nose and forehead then apply the bright red to her tender lips. She looked more cheerful with the colour on than the usual paleness of her mother's everyday life.

Finally, Nia chose a tiny, round compact of a creamy robin-egg-blue eye shadow. She loved the texture and bright colour. Her brows furrowed for a moment. What was she thinking? Despite knowing her father wouldn't like her wearing eyeshadow, she felt it made her look and feel glamorous. Being beautiful was only a make-believe concept for a stray with an address of Rural Route number two. Oh, how she spent hours daydreaming of a more prosperous life. Fancy dresses with ribbons and crinolines, black patent leather shoes, and even her own underwear with lace were only fantasies for this nine-year-old girl.

The bus that would take her back to the Township Line left the station only on the hour, and the five o'clock bus was the last bus of the day. Still wet, hungry, and very cold, she barely made it to the station and got on the bus with her remaining two dimes, clutching her tiny paper bag with the bright blue treasure.

It seemed like an endless ride home. It was past five-thirty, and Nia had missed supper. Her mother wouldn't have thought to save any leftovers for her simply because there never were any leftovers.

Nia's family was bustling around, quite unaware of her absence. Despite her lack of food, she felt delighted with the course of events that transpired that day. She'd managed the bus ride—all by herself. She took the risk and felt the fear. Nia handled the cold, wet process of getting to her favourite department store and now had the sheer pleasure of looking at herself with her bright blue eye shadow. Nia allowed herself to feel the glitz and the glamour of a Broadway star.

That bus ride was as transforming then as it would be throughout Nia's life. In fact, it was her first memorable demonstration of self-reliance, courage, risk-taking, compromise, and self-gratification.

It took a brave little soul that day to take the ride on the big blue bus. Nia found a few cherished moments of imaginary pleasure. Despite being hungry, that nine-year-old girl went to bed dreaming of her next bus ride.

CHAPTER 22

NIA, THE TEENAGER

Adele had a great deal of difficulty living alone on the farm since Jacque passed away three years earlier. She was in a bind, wanting to stay on her farm, but her adult children insisted she needed to go into the "old age home" after she broke her hip.

Nia was fifteen and saw this as an opportunity to create some distance between herself and the chaos of her family home. Flynn and Monique weren't too pleased with the idea of Nia moving to the farm to help her grandmother; Nia had become the necessary buffer for the household to survive daily eruptions. Nia wanted to help the now-failing woman extend her time on her beloved farm. Another advantage Nia saw was the one hundred dollars a month of reimbursement she'd receive for looking after her grandmother.

Adele's day was oriented around her meals, which Nia took great care to prepare. Soon into the living arrangement, though, Nia realized it was a relationship of service only without any grandmotherly love. Nia intuitively felt the absence of this woman's affections—never a hug, never a little kiss on the cheek, never a thank you. But what she did allow was Nia's boyfriend to visit.

In April of the previous year, Nia met Simon Windsor in front of the Bank of Montreal on Queen Street while she was out with a high school girlfriend. She had never felt such an urgent attraction to any young man before. She was in awe of his dark blue eyes, his blonde hair, and his strangely quiet and introspective demeanour. He was sixteen and went to a high school in the city. He showed a level of interest for Nia that she'd never experienced.

At the time, what seemed alluring to her was Simon's intent to pursue a girlfriend for an intense emotional coupling from the beginning. Given Simon's fervent attention toward her and her need to feel a sense of security in her tumultuous life, their young relationship jumped way past a fleeting teenager's crush to full-on believing they were in the forever kind of love.

Nia couldn't believe the voltaic permeation through her body when he first held her hand. Her sense of self felt encompassed by a power greater than herself. It seemed beyond magical for her as they strolled along the St. Mary's River in Clergue Park. The following weekend, the handholding progressed to the inevitable first kiss. It was Nia's first kiss too. Simon pulled her in and held her firmly with such great intention as if he was claiming her and wanting to own her from that moment forward. Nia's response was spellbinding, with her total submission to every muscular bulge of his chest and arms. She felt enveloped into his ownership, which she mistook for love.

Simon tied a red plastic pull string from the opening of a Dentyne gum package on the ring finger of her left hand. He spoke of marriage and wanting to be together for the rest of their lives. Nia felt blissfully overwhelmed. It was late, and it had been quite the evening in Bellevue Park. They'd spent most of the evening in his parent's car, headlights off, overlooking the other side from the Michigan sister city. Nia was obviously ruffled and flushed from necking. As the car pulled into her dirt driveway, she carefully removed the red plastic tie ring and placed it in her wallet before sneaking into her grandmother's house.

Nia lacked the life skills and emotional maturity to recognize the unachievable expectations involved with a relationship with Simon. She grappled with fear of disapproval.

Fear of disapproval from his father was Simon's own Achilles' tendon. His only life tool to stabilize himself and Nia was control, and he did this quite masterfully by the consequence of his piercing silent anger.

Nia first endured this crippling anger early one Saturday evening when they were supposed to meet to go to an eight o'clock movie downtown. His plan was for Nia to get off the bus at the stop closest to his house. She was supposed to walk over and meet him there. As the bus got close to her planned stop, Nia felt awkward and uncomfortable, knowing she would be interrupting their family dinner. She decided to go downtown and meet up with him in front of the movie theatre later. Nia waited dutifully in front of the theatre, and Simon finally arrived. Never before had Nia witnessed such silent rage, let alone it being targeted directly at her. There was absolutely no room for variation from his plan; regimented follow-through was the order, rather than any fluidity. The consequence was so extreme that Nia should've had the security and need for self-preservation to abandon any further relationship with that insecure, control-hungry young man. However, the opposite transpired. Nia demonstrated remorse, submission, and willingness to realign her actions rather than apply common sense toward establishing healthy boundaries and mutual respect.

Nia confused love with obedience. If she obeyed, her reward would be conditional affection, which really was masking the selfish need for his own acceptance and sexual interests. Nia quickly learned that her dutiful behaviour could elicit qualification, and it was the price of admission to this illusion of love and security that she desperately sought. She confused her attachment to Simon with love for him.

Simon saw Nia's appeasement and the wrapping of herself around his little finger as confirmation that she could conform.

He saw that Nia could rid herself of the life she knew and replace it with the right way to live (his way). Her emotional immaturity, along with an unstable, chaotic home life, made anything else seem desirable. Nia's insecurities made her an easy catch for the emotional gratification of one needing to possess another.

Given that Nia was raised with the Catholic teaching of sex being only for procreation and anything else was considered unholy fornication, she had great difficulty honouring Simon's different approach, which seemed to be completely opposite. Nia's grandmother, Adele, appeared to essentially be asexual following her fulfillment of her duty in that regard. She shed anything womanly—sexual or otherwise—and even appeared masculine in her features, including the long white facial hairs that she seemed oblivious to.

Nia saw her other grandmother, Etta, similarly and be-lieved she was quite content without sexual relations with her husband once they'd produced a child—Nia's father. While Nia knew her grandfather adored his wife, she was aware Etta would rebuff any of his overt affectionate gestures. Both of these women conveyed the same message to their husbands: their "duty" to engage in the unpleasantness of the sexual act had been fulfilled by giving birth, thus fulfilling God's expec-tations as well. The impression Nia got from both women was that sexual encounters were unpleasant, embarrassing, and painful. The coping strategy both Nia's grandmothers used was emotional detachment and passive submission to the sexual requirement to get pregnant. Even the word "pregnant" was considered socially unacceptable in polite conversation.

When Monique learned of Nia's relationship, she repeated the direct message: "He is not Catholic!" "Don't even think you can come home pregnant." Her mother's rants gave Nia the consistent, without-a-doubt message, not to get pregnant. Sex was, therefore, a bad thing and a definite sin out of marriage. Of all of the Catholic teaching, this is the one Nia took most seriously. Virginity of mind, body, and spirit was the path Nia wanted to take. However, she was in a constant emotional battle with her beliefs and the demands of her boyfriend.

And so went the remainder of Nia's year at the farm. Adele's health deteriorated, and she finally had to go into "the old age home."

Just past her sixteenth birthday, Nia returned to living at home. She and Simon quickly established a weekend dating regime, which, of course, included intimacy. Nia continued to desire their lovemaking to be in small incremental amounts.

Simon's private collection of *Playboy* magazines influenced his attitude toward sex. Women needed to be responsive and submissive, never questioning their role to be physically beautiful, adoring, and readily willing to comply. Yet any sexual assertiveness on Nia's part would've been regarded as reprehensible and undermined her intension to be Simon's wife and mother to his children. As a result, their premarital sexual balancing act was conflicting, not mutually progressive as young lovers ought to be.

Remorse and self-loathing would set in. Nia would beat herself up with this sexual dilemma between the requirement of her religion's sexual abstinence and Simon's sexual needs. The fight was furiously fought, however, with the loser always being Nia's self-worth. Nia only knew self-compromise. Had her older sister taught her nothing? Lily was a master at getting what she wanted. Unlike her sister, Nia consistently met Simon Windsor's expectations like cellophane wrap. Nia lost herself in her attempt to wrap around his and his family's life.

CHAPTER 23
NIA GOES TO UNIVERSITY

Simon had already been at The University of Western Ontario for two years, becoming successful in his pursuits of mathematics, physics, chemistry, and quantum mechanics, ensuring he qualified to get into Engineering school.

Education was the real qualifier of their relationship's sustainability; it was a prerequisite to be accepted into a prestigious Canadian university and be exemplary at the task. This expectation horrified Nia, as she felt she would never measure up academically to Simon's mother's expectations.

Nia forced herself to dig in. Her life became regimented around obsessive studying, and if she wasn't studying, she was fretting about not studying. The craziness of her unrelenting mission paid off, though. Nia graduated high school as an Ontario Scholar, plus received a scholarship from Brescia at the University of Western Ontario for her first year.

The only good part about this award for Monique was that her daughter would be living in and attending a Catholic academic community. This dream, for a least one of her children, had finally come to reality. (Although she would have settled for both daughters attending Nursing School at Sault College, as Lily was already deep into her first clinical rotation.) This was the only reason Monique agreed to let Nia leave her home for the university in London, Ontario.

Nia loved the old stateliness of Brescia. She loved the fancy parlours on the main level, the cleanliness, and the quality of each refined and polished piece of furniture—a lifestyle that was foreign to such a stray. Nia began to feel a slight bit of privilege that she worked hard to achieve.

The Ursuline Sisters were an order of nuns whose purpose was to serve God through education. Living among fifty nuns delighted Nia; she had no idea they would give her a sense of security and belonging. Nia was a "Brescia Babe" and loved it.

Orientation week was full of surprises: from a kissing extravaganza with the young men from Huron College and the panty raid from the young men from Sydenham Hall.

Simon was taken aback by Nia's keen participation in the orientation week's agenda for the Brescia Babes and curtailed the enjoyment by calling it ridiculous and stupid. These offensive remarks quickly realigned Nia back to her submissive role.

Given the frivolity of the first week, the second week of actually attending the classes gobsmacked Nia into an invisible, lost soul from Sault Ste. Marie. From the buildings of the campus to the lecture halls, everything was oversized and overwhelming. Nia could feel the constriction of her every fibre. The result was paralytic fear caused by the realization of the true test and ultimatum for measuring up. It felt like the pouring of the cement for the foundation of the codependency with Simon.

The first semester almost defeated her. Nia would collect-call home to speak with her dad every night, asking him if she should abandon ship. Flynn, in his wisdom, refused to let her come home. What then felt like desertion from her father turned out to be a pivotal gift of direction. It was only after the midterm exams that Nia felt she could doggie paddle in the academic sea of exams. Her survival necessitated a life of devotion to study. Intense fear was the pervasive motivator to succeed.

Nia was grateful that Brescia Hall was on the outskirts of the huge campus. Within the walls, she felt a slim sense of nurturing. Nia's roommate, Yvette, was a recluse and thus felt a kindred spirit in keeping the chaos of the rowdy Caribbean girls away from their room for them to study.

In November of the first year, Yvette invited Nia to her home for a weekend, where Nia experienced the inner workings of a strict Catholic home for the first time. Yvette came from a traditional Hungarian family living in another waterway locks city, Welland. Her father was one of the last residential milk delivery men. Her paternal grandmother dressed in all black, from her kerchief on her head to the toes of her laced up frumpy shoes, and lived with Yvette's family. Her role was to make a pot of soup every day for the evening meal (as well, to keep the fear of the Catholic God alive and well in their humble home).

Monique was thrilled that Nia was getting an extensive in-doctrination into Catholicism with her university experience. She was convinced it was divine intervention taking place for her second daughter.

Nia's first year of her Bachelor of Science degree was completed in what felt to her like a blink of an eye. Her obsession with studying earned her a place on the Dean's Honour List and entitled her to more financial grants to pursue her academic life.

For her second year, Nia aimed big; she applied to medical school. Her life of poverty and insecurity fuelled her need to establish a profession that would be rewarding personally and keep the cupboards and the bank account abundant. It was a challenging school to get accepted into—hundreds applied for only forty-five positions. It was Nia's merciless study regime and her ninety-seven percent average that secured her one of the spots.

Medical school was gruelling, especially the human anatomy dissection class.

All dressed up in her new white lab coat and armed with her shiny new dissection tools, she entered the anatomy lab. The pungent smell of formaldehyde greeted Nia as she stepped inside the huge, windowless lab with body bags on individual waist-high cement platforms lining the room. Each student was assigned a number, which designated the student's place and the corresponding body bag.

Nia moved to her assigned number seventeen platform and somewhat anxiously awaited instruction. As the anatomy professor, Dr. Armstrong, entered, Nia internally fanned herself. He was one of the most attractive men Nia had ever seen. That gorgeous specimen was exactly the distraction from the grim but fundamental learning experience that would take place two times a week for the duration of the school year.

The anxiety in the room was palpable. Nia realized she had to be strong; from every fibre she stood firm in her stature, fighting off the urge to flee the stench and the academic expectations.

Before the students would be allowed to open the bags, Dr. Armstrong spent a great deal of time explaining the overall goal of the class. He spoke about how foundational the authentic anatomical learning of each muscle, tendon, ligament, joint, bone, nerve, and blood vessel was the very basis of the profession.

Dr. Armstrong emphasized the hard truth of his class as his preliminary statements and then progressed into the humanity of the course. He identified that each of the bodies must be regarded with reverence and dignity. The individuals volunteered their bodies to science and must be treated as a gift to education.

Nia needed that to give her an anchor in her state of feeling totally overwhelmed.

When it was time to unzip the grey body bag, Nia was aware of her quivering hand as she pulled on the zipper. Death and bodies had not been part of her life experience; she'd never touched a dead person before. Inside was a white-haired, extremely thin Caucasian female. The card inside stated the cause of death—lung cancer at sixty-three years of age— and had a ten-digit reference number.

After an honourable length of time, Dr. Armstrong suggested to the class that they might consider naming their cadaver to maintain respectable regard for the more than generous donation of their bodies. Nia thought that was an excellent idea and named her cadaver Annie.

After a brief pause, the dissection commenced. The first incision was predictably the most challenging. "Cut longitudinally down the sternum from the jugular notch to the xiphisternal junction." Nia took a deep breath of the pungent air and made her first attempt. Her very light touch of the fermented skin made only a scratch. After several attempts, the scalpel penetrated the toughened skin and negligible subcutaneous tissue. The next task was to peel the skin and subcutaneous tissues from the pectoral muscles.

Nia was relieved when the class was winding up. She cleaned up her instruments and folded up her lab coat in her assigned basket, realizing it was not a good idea to stuff the already smeared and smelly front panel of the lab coat with bodily tissues into the basket. What were her options? Nia realized she had had enough and wanted out. She stuffed the lab coat and headed for the door to the hallway for the long walk through multiple corridors till she reached the outdoors.

While it was lunchtime, Nia wasn't her usual famished self. She knew her hands were scrubbed clean as she reached into her lunch bag to find her shaved roast beef sandwich and, without any forewarning, puked.

CHAPTER 24

ENGAGED

Nia entered into her third year of medical school after a trying start to her second—which did improve after that first day of anatomy class. She was determined to succeed and relied on her inherited courage and resilience to soldier through it. She had moved off campus into a two-bedroom apartment only three kilometres from the University. Her roommate was an equally studious medical student. Simon lived in an apartment in a different high rise but within the same complex. The dynamics of their relationship were starting to change; Nia was more self-reliant and spent less time with Simon.

It was brand new for Nia to feel the subtle expansion of her wings. It had taken a long time, but she'd figured out how to roll and succeed in the realm of academia and university lifestyle. The days of fear of failure and emotional dependency on Simon for survival had diminished. As her growth in self-confidence was germinating, his control over her proportionally declined.

The new Nia didn't cling to him, which caused Simon great uneasiness; his fundamental requirements were being challenged and depleted. A dramatic correction occurred with a jolt of four little words: "Will you marry me?"

One Sunday morning in late September, Simon sprung the question seemingly out of nowhere, taking Nia by complete surprise. She awoke as usual on the weekends in his bed, thinking of what had to be studied that day and preparing to head to the Faculty of Medicine study hall on the main campus.

That simple question was completely successful in caving Nia's recent developments of self-confidence and self-worth. The newly woven threads of self-discovery and sufficiency were disregarded in an instant with the responding word of "yes." After a small discussion of timing for the union, Simon called Nia's father to ask for her hand in marriage. Flynn could feel reluctance in his heart when he said "yes" after his own fateful experience of asking for Monique's hand in marriage. He could still see the faces of the angry French cabbage farmers. Monique had figured out what was going on when Simon asked to speak to Flynn. When she heard Flynn say "yes," she was (just like her mother had been) pissed off. The path of mortal sin was once again rearing its ugly head; Monique's feelings of anger rather than happiness with the engagement were expected.

Despite knowing her mother's reaction, Nia felt like celebrating and cancelled her study plans to spend the rest of the day in the arms of her soon-to-be husband.

The excitement carried forward through the following weekend. Simon and Nia visited Nash's jewelry store on Dundas Street downtown. Together, they chose an exquisite engagement ring, unique with the centre stone being a deep blue sapphire and ten small diamonds surrounding the main stone. Nia absolutely loved the ring. Simon had been saving his Physics Lab Teacher Assistant money for over a year to buy it. As Simon placed it on her finger, the look he gave her was one of sincere love and devotion, which she believed unequivocally would last forever.

Later that evening, they discussed their future as being married students at Western before Nia would start working as a physician. Simon would hopefully be in engineering school. They had a plan, but the design, implementation, and quality control were masterminded unilaterally by Simon. And so was the essence of their love structure. Like the design of a bridge, there was no room for variation or error, or else it would collapse. He decided the two would marry ten months after the engagement on July 30, 1976.

Of course, there was the idealistic role model which all of Simon's clan revered as the perfect matriarch—his mother. She was the yardstick to which Nia would be measured. Simon's mother could cook the picture-perfect meal, keep the house in the epitome of cleanliness and order, and make the perfect bed (with the bed covers so straight and tight that Simon's father would show great delight in bouncing quarters off the bed). She knew how to press the perfect shirt, darn the socks, knit the sweaters, plus she also worked full time as an administrator in the old folks home on the highway.

Every day, Nia felt she had to measure up, to be just like his mother, to qualify for his favourable loving for that day. Simon's unequivocal expectation was perfection, and Nia dutifully attempted to conform to her future husband's expectations. She was holding on to the notion that when she married Simon, she'd find the anchor of security that was lacking within her own family. Nia tried to fit within his domain, but she was too naïve to see the inherent flaw in this marital path.

One of the high expectations (expressed through undertones and actions) was for Nia to downplay and essentially disconnect from her family. Simon held nothing back when criticizing her family as being "less than" in all regards. The expectation was essentially no contact. Simon was emphatic about her recreating herself in the mould of his mother, with only one element of difference; he expected Nia to fulfill all of his sexual desires.

Nia didn't realize at the time, but all of Simon's unrealistic and self-compromising expectations were just another form of her life's experience of dysfunction and insecurity.

The tasks were endless, and her ultimate compliance required an evolving regime of tactical testing to acquire his daily approval. Only then would Nia be allowed the next twenty-four hours evaluation. Of course, there was great emphasis on the job of keeping her man well entertained between the sheets.

CHAPTER 25
HERE COMES THE BRIDE

Nia found herself reclaiming her childhood fantasies and endless hours of a make-believe fairy tale wedding with herself being the most beautiful bride. Her daydreams took her to the happy memory of watching Disney's Cinderella movie with her sister, Lily.

One Christmas, Nana and Papa gave both girls the same beautiful bride dolls. Nia's beloved bride doll possessed the key to the portal of her seven-year-old self's most vivid imagination. She savoured the wonderful experience of reliving the splendour of Cinderella being the bride and dancing with her prince. Oh, how she loved that doll right down to every tiny detail. Each part of her dress was a visual and tactile delight. Nia loved to twirl the doll in the white satin gown with a full crinoline underneath and an overlay of lace with translucent sequins twirl and sparkle. A large satin bow adorned the back of the dress, with trailing ribbons underneath the long cathedral veil. The doll's head was crowned with an exquisite diamond tiara, and diamond and pearl earrings decorated her ears. On top of the lace glove, the doll had a large diamond ring on her left ring finger. Underneath the luxurious dress, she wore lovely white lingerie with blue garters holding up the thigh-high white silk stockings while diamond and crystal high-heeled shoes adorned the doll's petite feet. Nia truly loved her bride doll—it was her most treasured toy—that provided her with hours and hours of pleasure as she explored her child-like fantasies of being a bride.

In her recollections of the delight she took in her childhood play with the toy, Nia's serene smile gave way to furrowed brows when she realized she never named her bride doll. She tried not to dwell on that for too long; her features softened again when she shifted back to thoughts of her dream wedding. Suddenly, a feeling of shock came upon her when she noticed the Prince Charming in her daydream memory wasn't Simon. This realization appeared almost like a sign or a warning. Was Simon not her Prince Charming? In response, Nia quickly shut down the visuals in her trip down memory lane and refocused her thoughts on her reality.

Nia's thoughts shifted to her much anticipated, beautiful wedding gown. Patricia, her high school friend, was studying fashion design at Ryerson College in Toronto and had what Nia perceived as the epitome of fashion sense. Patricia helped Nia commission a senior fashion design student to draw some original wedding dress designs for her. Two weeks later, she was presented with several sketches. Without hesitation, Nia chose one with simple, demure elegance.

Nia's third year of medical school required her to complete an internship. Nia's roommate was in Toronto for her internship, leaving Nia to have the whole apartment to herself. This was the only time she'd ever lived alone. Nia quickly discovered that she loved the quiet, empty apartment, free from the demands to please anyone else.

Simon was busy back home, finalizing the wedding details. Nia was perfectly content to let that happen. She was pleasantly surprised at his earnestness to have the process roll-out (his way) perfectly.

Nia was lucky to get an intern position at University Hospital on the neuroscience floor. It was always heartwarming and memorable to be present in that first moment when a patient would open their eyes after cranial surgery. The trust each patient gave her made her proud in her chosen career path. She never took for granted the connection between doctor and patient. Sharing in those moments and early days of their recovery, and then to actually see them walk out of the front door with their family, reminded Nia that she loved her new profession. The work she did fundamentally mattered. Every day, she would go to her internship, excited to have the opportunity to make a difference for the patients and her health care team.

Nia was sad when her internship ended but felt she'd made a positive impression with the neurosciences medical team. A position in that department after graduation would've been perfect for Nia and their marriage. Now, if only Simon could get accepted into engineering school.

Nia returned home one month before the wedding. There wasn't really anything for her to do since Simon had shouldered that responsibility. Patricia was busy sewing the gown, which was a truly unique design. The dress was ivory satin with a soft, high neckline that transitioned into a sheer ivory fabric, revealing only a hint of the tender young bosom beneath. The sleeves were long and made of the same sheer material that concealed the top of her chest. The full-length, A-line skirt was accented by a small ruffle of satin at the bottom. Cascading down the back, a line of twenty tiny, loop-holed covered buttons cinched the dress to Nia's form. The headpiece had small ivory pearls outlining the Juliet cap with a cathedral-length veil trailing behind. The dress was magnificent, and Nia couldn't believe it was hers, thanks to her wonderful friend, who had made it happen on a shoestring budget.

Simon chose an ivory tuxedo to match his bride. Their wedding was going to be all Nia had dreamed of as a little girl. She wanted to believe with all her heart that Simon was the man of her dreams and that their deep love would always carry them through life together.

On the wedding day, Nia was helped into her gorgeous gown by her mother, who appeared to be lost in thoughts of her own untraditional wedding. Nia was willing to share these moments with her mother, albeit vicariously. Once the final button on the back was fastened and the headpiece placed on top of her waist-length blonde hair, she felt like her reality reflected in the mirror was far better than any of her childhood dreams.

As she gazed into the mirror, Nia smiled at her reflection, pausing to absorb the moments of grandeur that she'd only imagined and believed she would never experience again. She truly felt radiant and fully accepting of all of her imperfections—her deformed but functional feet and the fact that she'd never have the striking face or figure of Lily.

Nia could feel her mother's attempt at a sincere hug but wasn't convinced of Monique's acceptance of this impending union. Neither Monique nor Simon put any effort into building a wholesome mother-in-law/son-in-law relationship. Both only went through the motions, which made sense given their mutual dislike of each other.

From Monique's perspective, marrying Simon was the wrong choice. She felt the pending complications she'd endured from her own marriage outside of her faith and the lifetime of trying to get back into God's good graces.

For Simon, Nia's family was inferior, and he made them feel uncomfortable in his presence. It was as if he and his family were making a grand exception to let a Catholic girl from Tarentorus become one of them.

Monique was uneasy, while Nia chose to just ride with it.

The bridesmaids toasted Nia with chilled pink champagne in beautiful fluted crystal stemware from Nia's wedding china collection. All giggly from the champagne, the bride and her seven bridesmaids dressed in their baby blue long gowns left the bridal chamber to catch their rides to the church.

The ride to the church seemed exceeding long, especially to Flynn, who drove Monique and the bride in his dad's new car.

The nervous, anticipatory energy was palpable from Nia's chest, but she tried to focus on the beautiful, windy, sunny afternoon. She continued to gaze out the window as they pulled into the church parking lot, recognizing most of the cars.

Inside the church, Nia caught a glimpse of the seated guests and heard the organist and the vocalist before she was wisked away to the vestibule. The large double doors were closed tight, but Nia imagined both of her grandmothers under God's roof, both being less than tolerable in their glances toward each other. Etta was inevitably wound up tighter than a drum, and Adele was happy to see Etta squirm in her seat.

Nia primped her gown to have the veil draped perfectly from behind. Her bouquet of coral sweetheart roses and baby's breath flowers was so delicate and fragrant. She chose to find a place of comfort between her mom and dad but knew the only thing pleasing her mom was that she was going to finally have the experience of walking down the aisle with her husband with their cherished daughter between them.

Flynn, too, was feeling nervous about having to formally detach from his governing role as father and give his beautiful daughter to a man who he knew to be subtly but absolutely establishing a clear boundary between Nia's family and his. Flynn knew whatever thread of his family union still existed would soon be severed at the end of the aisle by the man who had no interest in developing a relationship with him and only had token respect for himself and his family. Flynn was also feeling anxious for his beloved daughter, who actually gave him no stress in life other than at the beginning with her deformities. Flynn wrestled with this emotion of having to detach and recognized that his heart was heavy, and he didn't want to let go.

Monique was oblivious to her husband's apprehensions and began praying. "Hail Mary, full of Grace. . ."

The doors were still closed, but Nia could tell by the change in music, it was time. To run!

Fighting off her unconscious, her intuition, or however else one chooses to describe the inherent gut feeling, Nia resisted the urge to bolt. Saved or captured, one could debate. Once again, all of her discernments were eclipsed by Simon's alluring deep blue eyes encapsulating her. Nia's spirit may have taken flight, but her body moved rhythmically to the ceremonial wedding march.

The wedding was beautiful but in no way was the ceremony revered. Simon's parents and family loathed being in a Catholic Church, as did Nia's paternal grandmother. Regardless, Nia desperately wanted all the childhood fantasies of playing with her beloved bride doll to, at the very least, somehow infiltrate her real wedding. The ingredients were all present: the angelic dress, the flowers, the church music, and wedding Mass, the seven bridesmaids and seven groomsmen, the venue, the décor, the food, and the elaborate wedding cake. Already, Nia's family and friends felt distant, behind an invisible boundary separating Nia from the realm of her new married life. Nia somehow knew the little girl's fairytale wedding was put to bed forever.

The marriage was consummated, but it lacked the lost-in-love passion Nia fantasized about during her years of dating Simon. Nothing about their love making had changed. She somehow believed the Sacrament of Marriage would bless their lovemaking making it more bonding for them as a couple. The primal movements lacked the rhythm of meshing as in an intense tango of newfound, marital fusion. Simon wanted his new wife to perform sexually, fulfilling his fantasies.

For Nia, it was stone cold evident that there was no newfound union of mutual loving. There was no freedom or encouragement to be uninhibited in her expression of loving. This was the insidious onset of mutual discontent.

The next day, Nia didn't awake happy, enthused, or joyous. She only felt the unsettling churning of gravel in her gut, like cement. Quickly, she concealed her ill-at-ease state with a smile and kissed her husband good morning.

CHAPTER 26

NIA AS A MRS.

Nia took a passive role in her mother-in-law's house. Simon's mother lost no time in modelling the wifely duties Nia would be required to emulate to ensure her precious son was rightfully receiving. She made his pancakes, his lunch, and passed him his freshly pressed shirt, jeans, underwear, and socks before he ventured into his parentally purchased van to go to the last few days of his summer job.

Nia watched all of this, staying well out of the way of her mother-in-law while she was performing her wifely morning practices. Bacon was the standard measure of a start to a good day for the household. The breakfast table discussion oriented around the meals for the rest of the day.

By September, Nia and Simon returned to London to continue with their university education. As a married couple, they qualified for married student residence, a mere three hundred square feet of shared matrimonial real estate. Despite her unease with the marriage itself, it felt to Nia like it was their castle, balcony and all.

One of her first wifely tasks was to shop for the week's groceries at the familiar A&P store. The food she purchased was simple, and the items sparse, much to her new husband's chagrin. She didn't know how to create abundance, nor how to shop for a full refrigerator. She had the task but not the skill to manage meal planning for a week at a time.

The hammer fell when Simon asked her how much she'd withdrawn from the bank for the weekend; she happily conveyed twenty dollars. Nia was blindsided by the fury that followed. He quickly identified her supposed ineptness by not anticipating his financial needs (for what, she didn't know).

Their weekends usually consisted of walking and perhaps the Saturday night splurge at Mother's Pizza, for which twenty dollars would have sufficed. The limited quantity of currency was a huge error in judgement. From that time on, Nia wasn't trusted to create abundance. The reprimand was harsh, hurtful, and not forgotten. What she gleaned from this ill-treatment was the practice of walking on eggshells for the duration of her married life with Simon.

Simon's anger confirmed she was not in a loving marriage. He once again made her feel inadequate and like a burden. Unconditional love, affection, and nurturing were not in the cards for her.

The pressure of academically measuring up mirrored the challenge of the marriage. The former succeeded where the latter was never intended to meet success. The daily ritual of evaluating Nia's performance as a wife didn't give him the gratification he was seeking. He wanted their marriage to bring him a sense of emotional security and self-worth. In fact, that was the reason he sought marriage. Coming from a place of demanding power and control over his waif only produced frustration and discontentment for them both.

Happiness was a rarity in their tiny abode. It was a mandatory requirement to excise Nia's upbringing and any affiliation to it. This was more evidence of their corrosive marriage and her suffocated spirit.

Nia entered her last year of medical school, and it was indeed a struggle. It was crucial for her to stay focused and excel at her exams and clinical rotations.

For Simon, his school year was another year of a rejected application to engineering school. Now living together, it was evident to Nia that he didn't have his nose to the grindstone. When the letter of rejection arrived, he seemed shocked, as if his third year of applying entitled him to a place on the engineer roster. Nia couldn't understand his lack of ambition, which seemed to be preventing him from putting extra attention into his studying; he was always so close to acceptance.

Simon's father lamented about why his investment into Simon's education wasn't elevating him to the pivotal position of "My son the engineer." Both Simon and his father continually set themselves up by wanting the status, yet were unwilling to put in the extra effort to make it materialize.

This dilemma baffled Nia; her husband was the smartest young man she knew. As of the spring following their wedding, Nia had a job she loved and finally felt on top of the world due to her hard work, determination, and resilience.

In July of that year, they bought a Riviera Blue MGB sports car. Nia loved their new possession; however, Simon saw it as his own, and he dictated if and when Nia could attempt to drive it. It had a manual transmission, and she only knew how to drive automatic. As Nia practiced driving the car, Simon disparaged any shred of her driving competence. Her grinding the gears in an attempt to master a smooth shift perpetuated his fury. Simon's debilitating words and disgust seemed justified to him. His disrespect seemed necessary to teach his wife how to drive. His actions inevitably blocked her from having any success with her shifting. The result was a horrifically defamed and shamed Nia. The joy of owning a sports car became a submission to failure and fear of never being able to be a qualified driver. What possessed Simon to be so horrible? How could he be so malicious? On what basis entitlement did he feel he had to eviscerate her? Of course, there was never an apology for his actions. His displeasure continued in the form of deafening silence toward her. Each episode of failure strengthened his position of mastery over her. Simon quickly learned that anger was a highly effective strategy to keep Nia in line and submissive to his every demand.

One Saturday afternoon, the weather was perfect for a drive in the MGB with the top down. Thinking Simon was off with his brother, Nia came to the underground parking lot to find her gem, feeling ready to try driving by herself. Foolishly, she thought this might be allowed. The car wasn't in its assigned parking spot. Since Simon routinely washed and polished his car on the weekends, Nia walked up the ramp toward the front of the building, where he usually parked the car to polish it. Once closer, she discovered the front driver's side wheel was removed, and the vehicle was placed on a block. Unbeknownst to Nia, Simon was testing her. Like a well-primped cock, he demanded that Nia put the tire back on the car before he walked away.

Foolish girl! Why did she think today would be any different? Simon found sick pleasure in denying her.

Once again, belittled and maligned, Nia returned to the apartment, defeated, and cried into her pillow, knowing his fury would follow due to her lack of attempt to put the tire back on.

Predictably, it was a very short time into the marriage before the fantasy of her little girl dreams evolved into a progressive marital nightmare. Nia was served a daily dish of dissatisfaction as if it was her medication to stay humiliated into conformity. Her home life was task-driven, always under evaluation, and always with a failing grade by her husband. Yet every morning, she awoke to try it all again. Homelife was a droning passage. On the other hand, work was where Nia was encouraged, mentored, and felt she had something to offer to her patients, peers, superiors, and equally important . . . herself.

Nia had been working for almost a full year and married for almost two when an unexpected tragic event happened.

She'd been feeling unwell with a sharp abdominal pain that shot up into her right shoulder. The symptoms were apparently all indications of an ectopic pregnancy. A bikini incision was performed, and the right fallopian tube was excised, rendering her unlikely to have children.

It took a tragedy for Simon to take off his armour of control over his wife, and he showed her some compassion by holding her while they both cried. Literally, the young couple was ambushed by a little life lost. Despair was encountered for what seemed like an endless duration.

By Mother's Day of that year, Nia was consumed with the possibility of never having children. Then an unexpected "sign" appeared. A young boy handed her a single white rose while she was out for a walk. That gesture moved her into a place of faith.

CHAPTER 27
NIA, A MOTHER

B y the late summer of the same year, Nia was pregnant. A miracle had happened. Just as miraculously, Simon's stress and fear of losing another little life caused him to lighten his reproach of his pregnant wife. It was only then that she had a small taste of peace and contentment in their three years of marriage.

In May of 1979, the International Year of the Child, an incredibly beautiful baby girl, Aviana, was born. The young couple was awestruck. She truly looked like an angel painted by Michelangelo.

Reality set in when Nia's mother stated emphatically that, "Your baby is going to die!" This shattering statement stemmed from Nia's decision to breastfeed her baby. Monique's clinical approach resurfaced; she believed only in formula feeding a newborn. Nia intuitively believed Mother Nature knew better; what better way was there than a mother tenderly holding her babe, embracing the child in her body warmth while she filled her tiny belly with her mother's breast milk?

Nia's Nana cast further doubt: "You kiss that baby too much." Nia realized her way of tenderly cuddling and kissing the top of her baby's head while the infant breastfed was too much for her nourish-without-nurturing grandmother to bear.

Simon's kindness toward his wife was short-lived. With Nia no longer pregnant, the dynamics of his new nuclear family revealed to him another whole layer of her inadequacies. Fear of the loss of his baby seemed to fuel his sense of his own vulnerability. He didn't trust Nia with her manner of motherhood. Simon expected her to model his mother's perfectionism approach to childcare.

Nia felt trapped in the bowels of their new family dynamics. She felt herself becoming resentful of her husband's ability to devalue her as the mere maintenance department of their union. Simon and his infant's well being was to be Nia's primary care and concern; God help her if either were unhappy. Simon retained all the authority, while Nia was responsible for everything that came with having a new baby, especially the sleepless nights and dirty diapers. Of course, her natural sense of priority was to protect and provide for Aviana; Nia was a great mother despite Simon's unfounded, harsh judgements.

Understandably, Nia felt drained of all her faculties; fatigue and total lack of partner appreciation continued to suffocate her. Sadly, any opportunity to relax, revive, and celebrate her motherhood was simply not allowed. Despite this adversity, Nia loved her baby.

When Aviana was six weeks old, Nia's work friends invited her out for dinner; they recognized she needed a short break and missed her. She was excited to go and planned the evening away, ensuring she had a sufficient amount of breast milk pumped for bottle feeding with her dad. Simon reluctantly agreed as long as Nia had made dinner for him as well.

It was a warm June evening, and she chose to wear a white frilly cotton dress. Her body had resumed its tiny, toned abdomen; she felt attractive and enjoyed getting ready for the evening.

The inherent flaw in the evening's plan was that she didn't drive herself to the dinner party, thereby dependant upon her friends' timing for the evening to end. Unbeknownst to Nia,

Simon was fuming as Aviana was refusing the bottle of breast milk. Simon's ill mood escalated to anger, and even Aviana could feel his tension, which made her cry harder.

When Nia returned home after four hours of being away, she was greeted at the door by the horror of Simon throwing her into the concrete hallway wall. He lifted her by her neck, carried her to the bedroom, and threw her onto their bed with his hands clenched around her throat.

Nia's response to the hatred in Simon's eyes was utter surrender. Lack of oxygen forced her to forfeit completely when her body went limp. Perhaps that's what saved her. When Simon realized Nia had become lifeless, he released his grip, walked out of the room, and closed the door behind him.

The crying baby in the crib beside their bed brought Nia back to consciousness. Slowly, she collected herself and sat on the side of the bed, trying to muster the strength to stand and pick up her infant to comfort her by offering the babe her breast. Nia knew her husband was capable of immense emotional cruelty, but she never expected such physical abuse. (The trauma of his actions would be etched in her mind forever.)

Nia stayed in the bedroom behind the closed door with her infant until the next morning. Simon had already left for his squash game when she opened the bedroom door. When he returned that evening, he had no remorse for what had happened the evening before. The two ate their dinner in silence, and they never discussed the violent act.

The six months of Nia's maternity leave were coming to an end, and she would have to leave the blissful job of a full-time mother to resume her breadwinner role. She enjoyed her days of taking care of Aviana, who was growing into a well-nourished, happy, and healthy baby. Her beauty was undeniable, especially when she looked at her mother with her large, hazel-green eyes. Each playful day was filled with storybooks, songs, puzzles, and a multitude of toys. The children's songs like Anne Murray's "There's a Hippo in My Tub" and Raffi's

"Baby Beluga" played on repeat on the stereo. Nia was going to miss this time when she returned to work.

After Simon's fourth attempt to get into engineering school, he tried his hand at a teachers' college. He spent the year drinking Amaretto in a champagne glass with his legs slung over the side of the one armchair in the living room, complaining about the people aspect of teaching.

It seemed to Nia that Simon's lack of success was directly tied to his lack of ambition. He was ambling through life while she drove herself hard to be successful in her roles as a devoted mother and an excellent physician. Her dedication to both was undeniable and commended by almost everyone—her parents, his parents, her sister, her friends, but not her husband.

Nothing suited him about his life, and Simon took it out on Nia. Throwing Nia into the concrete wall that one night added to his power and control over her; she had reason to fear him. This worked out well for him in most areas of their married life.

Upon Simon's completion of his education at the teachers' college, they took a week-long family vacation back to their hometown of Sault Ste. Marie. Three days into their stay at his parents' house, Nia wanted to see her parents.

Simon's actions were in line with his need to demonstrate absolute control over his wife and her plans with his daughter. He responded to his wife's request by removing all four wheels off the car.

Fed up, Nia reacted boldly. She scooped up Aviana, grabbed the keys to her mother-in-law's coveted Impala, and sped out of the driveway. She knew her actions would have severe consequences. Simon would be furious with her. Her only saving grace was she hoped he wouldn't attempt to kill her with his parents as witnesses.

The thoughts of Simon's impending rage faded when Nia arrived at her parents' home and saw how tenderly they looked at their first grandchild. She knew her parents were being short-changed by her husband's need for control over her. She started to feel shame in her disloyalty and detachment from her family.

Simon's family's judgements continued to be harsh toward Nia's family, seemingly justified by their prejudices and a strong sense of entitlement. His family's words and actions intentionally minimized any significance of the other half of Aviana's genetic makeup and heritage. Their grandchild had exceeded their expectations, as her beauty was profound, and her personality was magnetic. This addition to Simon's "Windsor clan" was yet another source of elevation for them.

Despite Simon achieving the milestone of fatherhood, his father never downplayed his disappointment of Simon for not getting accepted into engineering school. Simon knew his father's high expectations of him were the source of his insecurities; nonetheless, he never dealt with his core issue of never being "good enough" in his father's eyes. Fear of disapproval and rejection fed Simon's resentment of his father. The spillage of the fear and resentment transformed into an angry young man. The one thing Simon was good at controlling was his wife, and he made sure she understood that daily.

By late summer, Simon was offered a science teaching job in Wawa, Ontario. Neither Nia nor Simon knew a soul in Wawa. Despite this, she dutifully resigned from her prestigious hospital job, where she had great potential for professional growth and development. With Simon finally employed, Nia was hopeful this would change his demeanour and their bank account.

Simon became a bit of a celebrity in the small town in Northern Ontario, as many of the parents wanted role models for their children. They wanted their teenagers to pursue their education to be able to seize the opportunities available in the forestry and mining industries. They need mentorship for their teens to avoid the lures of drugs and alcohol. As a result, Simon was leading the high life with no professional competitors to impede his parade.

Despite grudgingly accepting a job as a family physician in their new locale, Nia felt like she was silently suffocating in the frigidity of her own well-being. Notwithstanding the bleakness of her external factors, she once again found herself pregnant. While Aviana was a bright, busy toddler, going to daycare, Nia suffered from being pregnant and working in a position she hated. Her situation was insufferable, and she found herself frequently driving to her tiny office, pounding on the steering wheel in utter frustration.

Each lunch hour, she tried to go home to their small, third-floor apartment to eat, have tea, and start preparations for the family dinner.

After work, Simon would walk the short distance home and would eat the sandwich she'd made him, drink his tea, and then would lie down on the couch and play the same record at full volume: Meatloaf's "Two Out of Three Ain't Bad."

Nia hated that song and felt like it was salt in the wounds of her self-compromise. What was she thinking? Simon was never going to change. How could she leave him now that she was pregnant again and had a toddler? And so, she stifled her want of going. Like her environment, she felt frozen in her situation of entrapment. It was Nia's resilience and dedication to Aviana that got her through each day.

Thirty-six weeks into the pregnancy, Nia was ordered to go on bed rest. Simon had no interest in looking after his wife, so he made arrangements with his family to deal with the medical issue, shipping both Nia and Aviana off to Sault Ste. Marie. Avianna stayed with Simon's parents while Nia headed back to London to stay with a friend to wait out the duration of her pregnancy. This turned out to be a two-fold blessing; Nia was removed from Wawa's cold temperatures and her marital bed.

Two weeks overdue and with two stretch marks to prove it, Nia gave birth in total silence while Simon sat reserved and in judgement of even her ability to give birth. The medical staff in the delivery room were appalled at this father's lack of encouragement and compassion for his wife. Regardless, Nia held her healthy baby boy and felt her heart swell with joy.

Prior to Nia's discharge from the maternity ward in London, she was found to have a fever and was required to stay in the hospital for IV antibiotics. Between the fever and the fatigue of giving birth, she asked Simon to help her out of her sweaty hospital gown. He declined and felt the need to reprimand her for her awkwardness while she struggled to thread the tangled IV tubing through the sleeve of the fresh hospital gown. He gave her a look of disdain as he saw her stretch marks and postpartum abdomen. By the next day, she felt better and relieved to have an extra day of rest, a day to celebrate quietly with her new baby boy.

They had decided on the name Andrew. He was a beautiful baby boy but hungry as hell. After the usual few days postpartum, Nia's milk came in. Baby Andrew fiercely latched on to Nia's breast, then after a few sucks, would unlatch, scrunching his little face with anger at her as her milk let down like a geyser in his face. Both mother and child had to be patient to allow the milk flow to slow down before Andrew could latch on again and suckle to his heart's content. Nia couldn't help but giggle every time he would shake his scrunched up little face at his loving mother.

Aviana was thrilled to be a big sister, and she kissed her brother tenderly on the head. It was a common practice for Nia to nurse Andrew while rocking both of her children and read to them. The rocking motion and the warm blanket cuddled all of them.

Nia was at her in-law's home for a week before telling Monique and Flynn they had another grandchild. (Nia intentionally declined to tell her parents the news of her pregnancy when she visited them at Christmas, as her mother hated the idea of anyone being pregnant. She found it easier to conceal it from her parents because she was barely showing at the time and lived farther north and out of sight of her fretful mother.) They were happy but knew they wouldn't be invited to the Windsor's to see their new grandchild. Nia told them she would come as soon as she felt stronger.

With the addition of another baby, the isolation Nia felt in Wawa, and no job for her husband in Sault Ste. Marie, the family of four returned to London. Simon got a high school science teaching job where he felt like a minion rather than the king. Nia was thrilled to be quickly rehired at University Hospital.

As a result of their moving to London, Simon rented a small townhouse that Nia didn't see until the actual move-in day. Nia was excited for only one aspect of this new space; she now was the proud owner of a washer and dryer. Having two babies and a husband who played squash every day, she needed those tools and celebrated them in the form of a solo happy dance in the basement of their rental.

The expectations grew every day with the reality of the demands of mothering and being a physician in a teaching hospital (let alone a wife expected to make her husband happy continually). Nia endured the reality of giving her all to her family with zero appreciation from Simon. No affection or loving tenderness, just expectations of performance—including in the bedroom—only to disappoint him again and again.

One evening after the children were tucked into bed, Nia was yearning for some positive words from her husband. She was fresh from the bath, smiling at Simon as he lay on the bed reading *The London Freepress*. "Well, Simon. How do I look?" Nia was directly asking for a compliment because she never, ever heard any words of appreciation or kindness from her husband, and she wanted some. She figured she would have to ask for them if she were to get any.

Simon was not amused by the inquiry, even though he knew Nia accepted the imperfections of her birth defects. He didn't have it in him to throw her one small bone. What he did say was, "You aren't too fat, and you will never look good in stilettos."

And so their lives evolved with Nia knowing her place. A routine was established within the small family around the well-being of Aviana and Andrew. Nia loved her children and was delighted and in awe of their beauty, inquisitiveness, happy demeanours, playfulness, and energy, as well as their uniqueness. Despite her husband's constant petty criticisms toward her, Nia knew she was a good mother, fuelled only by her innate ability to love them by holding, feeding, bathing, reading, singing, and playing with her beautiful little creations.

At age six, Aviana learned the word "divorce" and what it meant from a little girl at her elementary school. Aviana begged her mother with such persistence and sincerity to affirm that divorce would never happen to them. Surprised at the question, Nia needed to respond to her daughter, if only to stop the repetitiveness of the question.

"No, Aviana. This won't happen to your Mommy and Daddy. We're Catholics, and Catholics don't get divorced." As Nia said these words, she knew how ridiculous that response sounded, but she had to reassure her troubled daughter, if only for the moment. Somehow, Nia knew that statement would come back to bite her in the ass.

CHAPTER 28

INFIDELITY

As Nia seemed so content in her mothering role, Simon distanced himself. It started as an evening with colleagues once a week. His mood would lighten on those days, as he was looking forward to his weekly work function. It began to seem odd to Nia that he was taking more time than usual to get ready for a colleague function. His appearance seemed to matter more to him as he would shave for the second time and applied cologne before his evening out.

To be honest, Nia also looked forward to his Thursday ritual out of the house because it gave her some time that wasn't constrained by his silent unrest. She had time to live without judgement for a few hours and go peacefully into sleep, knowing that he would come home late and not expect her to be awake when he returned.

This routine worked for them both for some time. However, Simon's "evening out" started to extend well into the early morning hours. Nia heard the front door open, followed by Simon going downstairs to shower. This seemed odd to her. *Why would he be showering now? He always showered in the morning, not before he went to bed.* One question led to the next inside her head. Nia got up to check things out. His clothes weren't dirty, and they didn't smell of smoke. His colleague, Jim, was a heavy smoker, so why wasn't there a smell of old cigarette smoke? She went into his wallet to see how much money was left or what dinner receipts he might have to explain his late whereabouts. She found no money in his wallet, despite knowing he had been to the bank machine that day. What she did find was some yellow lined paper, neatly folded in his wallet. As she unfolded the paper, a key fell out. On the inside was printed a name and an address:

Marilyn Connor
2079 Park Road
Apartment 612

Everything was suddenly very clear to her. Without a doubt, Simon was cheating.

The water turned off, and she heard Simon drying himself. Nia scurried back to bed and pretended she was sound asleep. Quickly after Simon came to bed, his breathing slowed, and she knew he was fast asleep. At that moment, Nia wanted to kill him. She could feel her weathered love for that man transform into the stench of loathing. The winds had changed.

The following Thursday night, Nia planned to execute her plan. She carefully prepared the last meal of the day for Simon, but there wasn't a response when she called him to come to dinner. The children were hungry and impatiently waited for their father to join them at the dinner table. Frustrated with Simon's lack of response, Nia decided to pick up his plate of spaghetti and meatballs and place it, still steaming hot, into the freezer. Without any hint of remorse, she proceeded to feed the children and enjoy her meal. Her dinner tasted especially delicious that evening.

When Simon finally came up from the basement recreation room, he was surprised that his food wasn't at his place on the table. Seeing his bewilderment, Nia stood from helping Aviana scoop her own vanilla ice cream and proceeded to the freezer to retrieve his food and place it down in front of him. His look at her was colder than his plate, and he angrily left the room to get ready for his rendezvous.

Nia continued with the usual routine of bathing the children, getting their pyjamas on, and reading each a story. Following storytime, instead of tucking them into bed, she fastened them into their seat belts of the old car. Simon had left a half-hour before, so she knew he would be at "Marilyn's place" already. The children didn't seem distressed by the change in routine and were happy to go on an evening car ride.

When she arrived at the address, her heart was racing. In the parking lot, she momentarily reconsidered her plan. It was dark, and the children were slumped in the back seat fast asleep, still in their seat belts. From the corner of the parking lot, Nia could see Simon's van parked close to the building entrance. The parking space next to the van was vacant, and she pulled into it and turned off the car. With the children asleep, Nia had the opportuny to expose his infidelity. The plan was cued up; all she had to do was play the next scene out.

For a brief moment, Nia wanted to abort the mission and retreat as if it was all a bad dream—but of course, it wasn't. She opened the car door and locked it behind her before proceeding to the entrance of the controlled entry foyer. With the lights at the building entrance and her car parked close, she could still see the children fast asleep.

Nia quickly found the name on the panel with the corresponding button. She pressed hard on the button without releasing it until she heard a female voice say in an irritated tone, "Hello? Who is it?" Nia responded with, "I know my husband's in there. Have him come down right now, or I'll come crashing into your door." Nia didn't get a response, so she leaned on the button again and again.

After fifty pushes on the button and no emergence of Simon, Nia headed back to her car. Seeing the children still sleeping, she opened the trunk of her car to retrieve his fishing knife. Fuelled by her wrath and anger, Nia slashed all four of his van tires. Shocked by her sweet revengeful actions, she drove home, amazed at her newfound inner strength to stay true to her mission.

After a period of quiet, Simon, still shell shocked by hearing the "caught in the act" voice of his wife, returned to the parking lot to find his slashed tires. Instead of his usual spontaneous eruption of anger, he stared at the destruction, dumbfounded and filled with a foreboding sense of fear.

The next morning, Nia awoke and went through her usual routine of getting the kids ready for school. She had called her boss and left a message explaining that she was sick and wouldn't be coming in to work.

When Nia was putting the kids and their school bags into the car, she could see that the van wasn't in its usual spot. An hour later, after taking the kids to school, she returned to the house and knew Simon had been there to change into his work clothes. Nia was relieved that Simon chose to sneak out before she returned.

It was nine o'clock, and Nia was ready to implement the next step of her plan. She called the locksmith and had every lock changed. Only she would hold the new set of keys. Nia then went into his den downstairs and smashed his Meat Loaf album collection with a hammer she had found by the back door. The house felt peaceful after the pile of destruction was left in the basement. She returned upstairs and searched the divorce lawyer listings in the yellow pages.

Nia knew she was finally done. She'd lost all trust in the man she loved since she was fourteen. The thought of him being touched by another woman revolted her into dry heaving.

By two in the afternoon, Nia was sitting in the lawyer's office. An hour later, she left the lawyer's parking lot with a solid legal game plan.

At three-thirty, the kids were happy in their seat belts, telling Mommy all of the excitements of their day as they made their way home. Life as they knew it was changing for them too. Nia had no way of saving them from this ordeal, but she had to make a choice. Simon had pushed her back against the wall only for both of them to discover the mother grizzly within.

By 5:00 p.m., the van, as predicted, pulled into the driveway. The kids were in their bedrooms playing: Aviana with her Barbies and Andrew with his race car set. Nia heard Simon trying his key in the front door over and over again. She then heard the rumbling and the cursing at the side door and then back to the front door.

The diatribe of obscenities continued, and the children came to find their mother holding her ground quietly in the foyer behind the solid steel front door. The kids realized it was Daddy yelling on the other side of the door. Nia knew this was going to be the hardest part of her plan. To Nia, she had little choice but to act quickly, as she knew firsthand how violent Simon could be. Despite their sad little faces, they didn't question the bizarreness of the situation and its uncertainty.

Still holding her ground without making any response to his deafening demands, Nia finally heard the van start up and pull away. Momentarily relieved, she took a deep breath only to turn and see tears rolling down the cheeks of her children. Nia crouched down to pull them into her, patting their backs. She explained to them that their Daddy and Mommy were unhappy with each other, and Daddy needed a "time out." There was no way she could concentrate on anything but staying on her course of separation. She'd have to learn how to be a single mother, even if it was by the seat of her pants.

After two weeks, Simon's anger turned into regret. He'd gone to a lawyer and signed over all his rights to the marital home and agreed to child support. Simon was hoping his efforts of goodwill would be enough to win Nia over, or at least for her to try forgiveness and allow him back into their lives. Nia had always done what he wanted, so why was this any different? Simon had never seen such fury in the actions of his wife. She wouldn't even release a suitcase of clothes for him. He realized his betrayal flipped Nia's characteristic submissive behaviour into a lioness, ready to kill him to protect herself and her cubs.

During the next few weeks, Nia was faced with the reality of managing her children and household alone. With great determination, she was getting the hang of the yard care and the maintenance of the swimming pool (albeit baptism by fire). She endured the shouts from the other side of the door saying, "There's no way you'll be able to stay in this house! The weeds will be up around your neck, and the pool will be dark green with algae. You'll never succeed, you stupid excuse of a woman!"

Nia met those words with the inner fortitude of a powerhouse. Simon was right; she had no idea how to do these things; however, she had the resilience to learn. After the kids were in bed that evening, she went into the pool house to start the pool backwash, only to have the lever come off into her hand. That was the final insult to injury. For a brief moment, she felt like caving in, like she couldn't find the strength to go forward into the wild, uncharted land of being a single mother with a big house, a big mortgage, and a big swimming pool to look after. Everything seemed too overwhelming.

She could feel the panic set in but realized that panic attacks pass and that she could right all of her irrational thoughts. She turned off the pump and turned off the light, went inside, and went to bed, knowing she could be resourceful after a good night's sleep.

The next morning, she called the pool company. They sent over their serviceman, who gave her the basic instructions to manage the pool with ease. He also replaced the lever. The pool guy quickly realized what was happening with this household. He didn't charge her for the service call, hoping she would call him back. Of course, she never did.

CHAPTER 29
NIA LEARNS TO PLAY

Nia had every other weekend off that first summer after her separation from Simon. The court granted him child access as the non-custodial parent. The kids missed their dad, and it was hard for Nia to see their sad faces while trying to navigate the territory between living with Mom and every other weekend with Dad.

Despite this emotional pull, Nia was beginning to feel her world lighten up. She decided to reinvent herself, to find out how exciting single life could be. Outwardly, there was no sign of a wilted flower. She began to feel an increase in confidence and self-worth. Nia wanted to exercise her new attributes.

From work, she had developed friendships with a few single women who knew how to party. Nia began to look forward to her every other weekend being wild and single, followed by being the fun mommy who had the kids' friends over to have fun in the swimming pool.

The summer lightened the emotional load, and Nia found herself dancing on the pool deck to Whitney Houston's new song "I Want to Dance with Somebody." Nia could feel herself getting into the moves, wearing her new teal coloured bikini. She danced with a huge smile on her face and didn't care if anyone was watching.

Over the next three years, Nia's activities became more expansive on the professional and personal sides; sometimes, she even blended the two. In 1988, Nia met her French lover in Houston at a neurosurgery conference where he was a keynote speaker. They met at a glamorous champagne reception in a posh hotel. Nia felt lavished by the fancy party with ice sculptures, caviar, and chocolate-covered strawberries. Servers silently moved about the room, ensuring everyone's champagne flute never reached the half-empty level. For a poor little girl coming from Sault Ste. Marie, that degree of glamour exceeded her childhood daydreams. There were the sounds of many languages, the elegance of the views, and a vast array of designer-dressed, beautiful people. The spectacle made Nia feel she was in a sophisticated movie scene. The event was surreal and foreign to her; however, she wasn't going to shy away from the opportunity to "taste" this rich experience.

Nia excused herself from her group of colleagues and moved toward a French group. She could hear the romance of the language while they were discussing where they would go for dinner following the reception. A man in this group caught her interest. In her black, off the shoulder, somewhat provocative evening dress with long ribband earrings, Nia could feel her simple beauty profoundly standing out in the crowd. Approaching the man from behind and allowing herself to move into his personal space, she whispered, "Bonsoir."

Without turning around, he knew there must be an intriguing woman behind him who certainly was not from France. "Bonsoir" was the first and last French he ever spoke to her.

"Hi, my name is Nia. I'm from Canada," she said, speaking into the back of his neck.

"Ahh, I love Canada, but their French is not so good," he said as he turned around, delighted to see such a beautiful woman before him. "It hurts my ears, your French-Canadian language," he said with a beaming smile on his face. "My name is Christophe, and I am enchanted to meet you, Nia."

"Have you been to Canada?" Nia asked, having no interest in his verbal response. She was much more interested in his body language and the allure in his voice.

"Ah, yes, Montreal," he replied, definitely wanting to keep the encounter going.

"Yes, Montreal is a beautiful city. I've been there a few times. I especially love the old part of the city." Nia had been there with her children, but she had no intention of referencing being a mother that evening. Nia wanted to seize this fantastic opportunity to display and savour mutual attraction with a foreign stranger. She'd turned on and turned up her enticing sensuality, as it was familiar and pleasing territory.

"It sounds as if you are planning to go out for dinner with your colleagues," Nia inquired.

"Yes, but my plans might change. I think it is with you I will eat. Shall we go now?" The French gentleman was anxious to take this rendezvous to the next level.

"Well . . . . Your friends might be disappointed that you're not going with them." Nia had no idea why she said that, as she, too, wanted to leave with her new French distraction.

"Ahhh, no. They are, how do you say? Envious." His reply was in alignment with his plan. He leaned into her, smelling her fragrance with silent acknowledgement and delight in her fresh, untethered nature. "Let us go from here. I want to speak English with you. I want to learn more about Canada. I do not want to be with French people tonight."

Nia nodded and enjoyed how he pressed his body against her side while holding her arm, leading her to the hotel lobby.

He motioned the doorman to hail a cab and opened the cab door for her.

As she readily slipped in, the only dubious professional thoughts in her mind were about the surface anatomy of this exquisite specimen.

"Ahhhh, you are so beautiful, not like French women. Your skin is so soft and, how do you say? Pink." He stroked her cheeks gently and touched her lips lightly, tracing their shape.

Nia used her subtle seduction, accepting his refined forwardness, and responded with a kiss.

He briefly detached from the kiss and angled forward to give the driver the name of a nearby restaurant. He returned to the kiss while caressing her blonde, shoulder-length hair. Once the cab stopped at yet another hotel, Nia had to unfold her legs off his lap, exposing the lace at the top of her sheer, thigh-high black stockings.

"I'm not really hungry after the reception," Nia said coyly. She wasn't interested in food any longer. She wanted to continue exercising her sensuality.

"Shall we drink?" he asked.

"Yes, I'd enjoy talking with you and learning more about you," Nia conveyed with a slight fluttering of her eyelashes.

A smirk grew on the Frenchman's lips. "Yes, to talk. Drink, what shall you like?"

Not knowing anything about French wines, Nia decided to stay in familiar territory. "Gin and tonic, please."

"Is this a Canadian drink? I do not know this gin and tonic."

The drawn-out "s" sound when he spoke made Nia feel giddy inside. "Not really. It's a drink my grandmother liked. Most Canadian men like beer."

"Tell me more about Canada. I want to know more about moose."

"Yes, we have moose," she said playfully.

"Ahhhh," he responded with apparent disinterest.

Nia could see he was no longer thinking of moose, and neither was she as she marveled at his dreamy eyes.

As the evening progressed and the gin and tonic glass was emptied, Nia's Frenchman rose from the table, taking her by the arm to the foyer, where he hailed another cab. Nia knew the next location would be his hotel. The passion was intense while travelling to the next destination. The newness of the encounter was outlandish to Nia, but she leaned into the experience, knowing she would be open to it.

The cab pulled up to the entrance of yet another beautiful hotel. With an air of natural sophistication, he said, "Cointreau" to the bartender, as he held up two fingers. Two liqueur glasses were handed to him, which he held in one hand. His leather bag containing his research papers was slung over his shoulder as he looked at Nia. She knew this was her final opportunity to change her mind—or not.

They got to his room on the top floor of the massive hotel. The evening light softly filtered through the room. Nia's only decision that night was whether or not to enter her lascivious side with the full intention of experiencing its uncharted land. The bags were put down on the chesterfield, and the Cointreau placed on the side table by the enormous bed.

Nia let her lioness within take his arm and led him into the massive white bathroom with the glass shower. Still fully clothed, she could see her reflection in the full-length, mirror and she approved of the diva looking back at her.

Nia reached in and turned on the shower. She pressed her finger onto his lips, signifying that he was to follow her lead.

When Nia was weakened with splendour, he turned the shower off and wrapped her in warm, luxurious white towels. He carried her to the bed and threw back the white linen duvet. Without missing a beat, their intimacy continued deep into the night.

Early the next morning, she laughed while hearing the shower running and her French lover singing, "Oh Canada."

Even though Nia's French connection was short-lived, it was the pivotal point in her knowing she was not the sexual disappointment Simon made her believe throughout their marriage. She had proved to herself she was a beautiful, sensual, and sexual woman. Nia knew she desired an attentive, appreciative, sensual, and sexual man. Her French lover was all of that and more.

CHAPTER 30
NIA MEETS FERNANDO

Nia met another alluring man in a bar in London. She was out with her cousin, Alice, having a marvellous time, both enjoying the freedom of the single life. Live music played, and the two were happy grooving to the tunes when four men approached their table, wanting to sit down. They'd been watching Nia and Alice beaming with whatever they were discussing.

Alice had been living with Nia for approximately six months following her own divorce. Nia opened her door to her dear cousin, knowing the pain of having an unfaithful husband.

Alice was devastated when she first arrived at Nia's home; she felt eviscerated to her core. For the first week, Alice couldn't eat, sleep, or walk. Nia physically had to help her with all of her basic functions. Over time, they helped each other heal from the emotional abuse their husbands both felt entitled to deliver.

On that evening in June 1989, the two beauties were in a fine, playful mood. Nia was excited because she was about to embark on another rendezvous with Christophe in Cincinnati. The thirty-something-year-old bachelor group were obviously attracted to the lovely ladies. The four of them didn't intimidate Nia or her cousin in the least. As the evening transpired, the playfulness continued. Nia's attention was drawn to one of the four men, Fernando, primarily by his notable ability to be multilingual. The interaction that evening was frisky and highly flirtatious. Both Alice and Nia could serve up outrageous and funny innuendos like a tennis match while the bachelors kept turning their heads from one banter to the next. The boys were putty in their hands, and the two cousins ruthlessly toyed with them.

For the next few Saturday nights, the playful bar bantering continued. By the end of the July-long weekend, Nia and Alice decided to have a pool party at Nia's home. Aviana and Andrew were with their dad for the entire month of August, and they had left earlier that Saturday morning. (Nia was very careful to keep her children away from her dating life. It was now three years since the end of her marriage with Simon. She and the children were well use to the pattern of Mom's time and Dad's time over the course of each week, school break, and holiday.)

The four bachelors arrived at the pool party in a limo, obviously excited to be invited to Nia's pool party.

The bachelors couldn't believe the grandness of Nia's residence and were curious about her living situation. Of course, Nia kept the party playful and didn't indulge in their curiosity. She and Alice just wanted to continue their teasing banter in their exquisite bikinis in the candlelight of Nia's backyard, not answer serious questions about their pasts.

Nia loved the male attention she never had from her first marriage. As she dashed into the kitchen to get more ice, she noticed her reflection in the hall mirror. The flow of her long blonde hair, her fucia lips grinning, her very sexy teale coloured bikini, and a demeanor of glorious playfulness made even herself surprised at her own radiance.

That's how Fernando Santos and Nia started on such a playful note. Fernando had never had a serious love relationship in his adult life. Being the eldest in a traditional immigrant family, it was his duty to lead the family and future generations into a respected, higher quality of life. As a result, Fernando focused on only two areas—his education and hockey. His keenness for both became obsessions that he couldn't detach from when life happened.

Nia misread the warning signs concerning Fernando. (She should've known better!) He displayed no ability or intention to interact with maturity and interdependence as in a healthy, lifelong partnership versus a co-dependent relationship in an unhealthy relationship as she had with Simon. Ultimately, that's what Nia wanted and needed. She should've kept herself open to future opportunities when such a man would find her.

Unfortunately, this wasn't the case for neither Fernando nor her. Nia naively believed she could "fix" Fernando. He naively coasted into her domain, soaking up her abundance of love and care without giving any need for his own emotional maturity and development.

Fernando Santos was easy for Nia. He was the polar opposite of Simon. She had grown emotionally but was thrown off by her own bit of newly acquired independence and ego. To Fernando, she hit all the "features" he was looking for in a woman: beautiful, slim, well educated, financially independent, homeowner, and well employed. The only negative features he saw with Nia were that she was a divorcee with two children.

Despite the later two features, dating progressed happily for both of them. Nia loved fitting into his Portuguese family. Even though she knew she didn't meet his parents' preconceived ideas of what their firstborn's possible intended spouse might be. They almost immediately started loving her for her genuine magnetism. Unbeknown to Nia, Fernando was delighted Nia was Catholic.

For Nia, it was very different than her relationship with Simon's family. There was no judgement or arrogance, only acceptance, inclusion, and family fun. Her relationship with Fernando progressed into a comfortable rhythm for both of them. Every other weekend, the children would be with Simon. On those weekends, romantic, indulgent pleasures were the consistent theme.

After a year into the relationship and a gradual introduction of Avianna and Andrew to Fernando, Nia's family dynamics started to get a little blurry for the children. Fernando began coming for dinner on school nights, helped with homework, went with her and Avianna to Andrew's hockey games (which really pissed Simon off). It progressed into sleepovers on school nights.

Nia could tell the children were overhearing things at Simon's place about Fernando by their innocent questions to her. "Dad says your shacking up. What's shacking up?"

Nia was beginning to become rattled by her core values of her children coming first. Things with Fernando had to change. It was September 1990, and there was a Portuguese family wedding pending. She and Fernando had a wonderful night of dancing, eating delicious seafood, chocolate desserts, and drinking amazing Portuguese wines. This was the first time that Fernando's extended family had the chance to meet his much talked about "namorada." Nia didn't disappoint. She wore a rich red evening gown in her usual grandeur of subtle elegance oozing of sensuality. She and Fernando held an audience while they swayed on the dance floor and schmoozed each family table almost as if they were the bride and groom.

Following that Portuguese family wedding, Nia felt such acceptance, love, appreciation, respect, and attention from Fernando's family. It was coming down to a crossroad for her and her children. She knew she didn't want a live-in "boyfriend" to be in the mix with her newfound independence with her children.

She felt she no longer had clear boundaries where her children were totally separate from her dating life. Nia began to put more thought into this relationship, knowing her family values were of utmost importance to her. Nia decided to talk about these values with Fernando and suggested they take a break in the relationship.

Fernando was quite blindsided by this discussion. Everything was going his way. He thought he had a gorgeous, sensual woman, who loved to cook, adored his mother, and was financially independent, but suddenly she was talking about taking a break. Fernando was visibly taken aback by her wish and, without further discussion, calmly said goodnight.

The weekend passed, and Nia couldn't tell if she was relieved or regretful of wanting to take a break from Fernando. What she realized was she missed her alone time to recharge her batteries.

Over the course of the next two weeks, life resumed its normal flow. Nia was somewhat surprised the kids didn't raise the topic of Fernando, and neither did she.

CHAPTER 31
MARIA AND CARLOS

Maria had grown up in Porto, Portugal, and immigrated to Canada by ship passage across the Atlantic to Halifax's Pier Twenty-One in January 1953—when she was only nineteen. She had chosen to come to Canada to join her fiancé of three years after maintaining their engagement by mailing romantic letters monthly.

Due to persisting post-war economic hardships, Maria's family immigrated to Brazil, which meant staying in Porto was no longer an option for her. She grappled with her choices before using her fiancé's money to purchase transport to Canada. She traveled by train from Halifax, Nova Scotia, to London, Ontario. She descended the train to fierce winds taking her thin coat up past her waist with the hemline whipping at her cheeks. Clenching her coat collar, she saw her fiance, Carlos Santos, rushing toward her, bearing a bouquet of red carnations. (She would've preferred red roses but considered that perhaps Canada didn't have any roses.) Maria appreciated the gesture and the deep kiss, instantly heated by his embrace.

Carlos scooped up her small suitcase and whisked her to an old Chevy Suburban borrowed from his uncle to pick up his soon-to-be bride. He drove the short distance from the train station to the courthouse. Maria didn't realize her day of arrival would also be her wedding day. She assumed they were going to an official office to have her immigration papers reviewed.

Flustered and quite taken aback, Maria excused herself to the dingy restroom to splash cold water on her face. Looking into the mirror, she saw a tired yet exhilarated beautiful Portuguese woman in a land that was cold and bleak. Maria quickly realized she had no alternative but to proceed with her intended's plan.

In only her travel clothes, the bouquet of red carnations tied up with a white hair ribbon retrieved from her purse was the only bride-like adornment she had. As she returned from the restroom, Carlos caught her eye and gave her the most captivating smile. Believing in his love for her, Maria proudly walked with him toward the Justice of the Peace to pronounce them husband and wife.

After the civil union, Maria and Carlos Santos sat in the back in the old Chevy while Carlos's uncle drove. She was caught up in the delight of the wedding excitement and was looking forward to their next stop.

As Maria stepped out of the car, she noticed Carlos's facial expression turn as bleak as the weather. The couple entered through the back door to a small kitchen chock full of Portuguese people of varying shapes, sizes, and ages. The gleeful sounds abruptly ended as a tiny, hunched-over older woman dressed from head to toe in black entered the room. Carlos must have stepped away because Maria, still with her coat on and her bouquet of carnations in hand, faced the woman without him at her side. The elderly woman approached Maria and reached for her face with her old, cold, skinny hands. Her sunken eyes stared directly in Maria's, and the two stood eyeball to eyeball. Her fierce, penetrating glare chilled Maria to her core.

And so, this was the beginning of Maria's married life in London, far from the loving arms of her family now located in an equally foreign land in South America. The head of her new family was certainly not her husband. He was the eldest of his six siblings, all sisters. Carlos was the breadwinner for this household filled with Portuguese estrogen. All the sisters were jovial and thrilled to have Maria fill their house with her happy songs. Her mother-in-law certainly didn't share the sentiment.

Maria had only two purposes; to care for the matriarch of the family and to make babies. By February 1954, it was clear she was fulfilling her obligations and gave birth to her cherished firstborn, Fernando. Immigrant mothers were given a choice to stay in hospital once stabilized or not given the language barrier. Maria wanted to go home because she didn't understand or want anything to do with bottle feeding her Fernando. Nothing gave her more pleasure than to hold, breastfeed, and sing to her beautiful baby boy. She realized this was her purpose in life and wholeheartedly embraced being a mother.

Throughout her restricted life, Maria maintained some self-sustaining joy in her heart, powered by an unlimited abundance of love. Resilience and her unwavering dedication to her family were reasons why Nia willingly entered Maria's family.

Nia could see the all too familiar parallels between Maria's wedding and her mother's. Religion was the common denominator. For both of them, there was the huge disappointment of not having a full Catholic wedding. Similarly, they weren't able to freely practice their lifelong devotion to being Catholic. Maria was forced to live an unconscionable life where she couldn't even baptize her babies in her faith. Her now widowed mother-in-law, once a Catholic, converted to Jehovah's Witness shortly after she immigrated to Canada. For some dark secret that she held up in her vault of solid convictions, she drastically changed her faith. Hell had no fury like the antagonism of Maria's four-foot-ten, hunched-over dictator of a mother-in-law.

CHAPTER 32
WEDDING NUMBER TWO

Fernando was not doing so well on his home front. His mother knew something was off the very first night when he came home on a weekend night. "What's wrong? What did you do? Is Nia ok?" Each day became more miserable for him and his family.

It was Friday afternoon of their third week apart, and Nia was checking on her last few patients before heading off for the day. She heard her pager go off and went to the telephone.

It was Fernando. "Hi, it's been a few weeks. I miss you. Can I take you to the Hunt Club for dinner tonight?"

Nia was getting a little bored. She needed an evening of dining and dancing. Was she starting to miss Fernando? Was this a good idea? She was asking herself these questions, but she didn't have a good answer in that moment for either of them. So, she frivolously said, "Yes."

The evening was exquisitely curated (likely by Fernando's brother as Fernando didn't have the talent or interest in such detail). After the delicious dark chocolate covered strawberries and cappuccinos, Fernando stoically stood up. He reached for Nia's left hand, got down on one knee, and said, "Nia, would you please be my wife?"

Nia was shocked. She hadn't seen that coming. She thought the relationship had taken a turn to go in separate directions. A proposal was truly a giant step for Fernando.

While all these thoughts were steamrolling through her head, he presented her with the most exquisite diamond ring she'd ever seen. "Yes, Fernando, I will marry you." The words rolled off her tongue as if unexplainably, someone else was speaking for her.

For her second marriage, Nia's wedding dress was more glamorous than demure. Elegant lace adorned the front top of the gown, extending over her shoulders down each arm, coming to a gentle point on the back of each hand. Small, pearl glazed, white sequins embellished the lace, which gave a mother of pearl illusion in evening lighting. Cascading from the fitted, tiny waistline (lending no evidence of the previous pregnancies), tiers of ruffled tulle adorned with the same pearl-lustred sequins scattered throughout the full length of the skirt.

Nia clearly had no fear of displaying her newfound beauty. She was proud of her strength, courage, confidence, independence, and, without a doubt, her sensuality. The backless gown embraced these attributes, dramatically exposing the exquisiteness of her slender anatomy dipping down to the small of her spine. The ultimate adornment was the draping of seven strings of pearls across her back. The front of the gown looked haute couture, while the back of the dress was unquestionably breathtaking. Nia felt as radiant as she looked.

It wasn't until the limo ride to the ceremony that Nia's mother and father met Carlos and Maria and discovered their destination wasn't to a Catholic church.

"What?" Never had Monique experienced a Portuguese family that wasn't Catholic. Flynn gave Monique a stern look; this wasn't the time or place to react to the piece of information that was important only to her.

Despite the disappointment over the wedding's location, Monique (like Nia) was immediately taken with Maria's warm, loving nature. The five shared friendly conversation on the ride to the church, which helped ease some of Nia's nerves.

Large, fluffy snowflakes settled down around Nia as she walked from the limo holding the skirt of her gown high. The snowflakes glistening, in harmony with the lustre of her sequins, gave her the illusion of an enchanted queen. Winter was definitely Nia's favourite time of the year. What better time than the festive spirit of Christmas to have a wedding?

Nia proceeded down the aisle, stunning those attending with her radiant grace and elegance. At the front of a non-denominational church, her soon-to-be husband resumed his anxious state, looking to his bride for some calming reassurance and encouragement.

Some of Fernando's nervousness faded as he met her gaze in the tiny church packed full of people they loved. He watched his bride approach, flanked on either side by her parents.

Nia could feel the tentative grip of her father on one side and the vicarious glory of her mother, once again, proceeding down the aisle, savouring the experience as her own. Recognizing her mother's desire, Nia willingly shared her stage.

Nia did love this man. She walked down the aisle, this time without hesitation. It all felt right (at the time). After all, Fernando was easy to love and understood the idea of freely giving love.

Fernando believed Nia's affection and nurturing toward him was seamless, especially after their weeks of separation. The real cherry on the cake for him, though, was the love that existed around them: her love for him, her children's love of his family, and their mutual love for Nia's. Nia and Maria fit like a right hand to a left hand. They loved each other and respected each other, given that they shared the same core values. Maria and Carlos didn't take issue with Nia being a divorcee with two children, marrying the first son of a traditional Portuguese family.

To Nia, Fernando was atypical; he didn't have any residual emotional baggage from previous relationships, nor did he have any children. He seemed like a clean slate. At the beginning of their relationship, Nia found it interesting to have a man who was almost forty and had never lived outside of his mother's hearth. Nia's naïveté at the time of her wedding precluded her later wisdom that his state of emotional maturity or manhood beyond self would never change.

CHAPTER 33

APGAR OF ONE

As their life together progressed, Nia deeply wanted to have a child with Fernando. Intuitively, Nia realized she had an abundance of love to give and wanted nothing more than to be a mother again. Within their first year of marriage, she was pregnant.

On September 4, 1992, Nia was chairing a high-level meeting at the Faculty of Medicine. Nia had been very happy earlier in the day; it was the first day of her wearing a maternity skirt and fashionable white blouse. She thought she looked pretty hot for a pregnant lady.

Nia desperately tried to stay focused and in command of the agenda at hand. But the day took a dramatic shift south. She started to feel low back discomfort that quickly grew into an ache and then pain that she couldn't ignore. Shifting her body repeatedly in the chair at the head of the boardroom table gave her no relief.

When the meeting adjourned, Nia proceeded quickly to her car to drive homeward. She felt she was on automatic pilot driving home.

The pain came in waves, and at the height of each wave, she felt her abdomen writhe. She was stuck in bumper to bumper traffic on what seemed to be an endless ride home. She couldn't focus on anything other than the pain to be able to navigate to a different route. Dread filled her as she contemplated the inevitable grievous turn of events. She finally got to her driveway and could see that the pool closing crew was just leaving. Nia was too distraught to deal with pool issues and simply excused herself to go inside.

A brief moment of relief washed over Nia when Aviana and Andrew were home from school to greet her. All she needed at that moment was to hug them to feel secure and regain her strength and fortitude to deal with what was transpiring. No words were exchanged; both children instinctively knew their mother was suffering, and they needed to rally around her. Aviana led Nia to her bedroom—she was grateful to lie down—and then took control of the situation by calling Fernando to tell him he needed to come home immediately. Andrew didn't leave her side the entire time.

Nia closed her eyes and rolled from side to side, unable to find a place of comfort to rest. She couldn't drink the cup of tea Aviana brought her, nor could she manage the words to say thank you to her children.

Aviana and Andrew kissed and hugged their mother; both had tears in their eyes as they said their quick goodbyes and got into their father's van. Nia felt some relief in knowing they'd be ok while she attempted to deal with this cruel hand of life.

Fernando arrived with a deep look of fear in his eyes. The seemingly long drive to the hospital was without words, but their hands remained tightly interlocked as Nia's pain amplified.

The silence lingered even as Nia guardedly and bravely exited the car. They headed directly to the third floor of the hospital—the maternity ward. Her two previous trips to this destination were joyous, not with the weight of foreboding sadness.

Fernando spoke to one nurse while another led Nia to a private room at the very end of the long hallway and helped her out of her pretty clothes. Warmed blankets were placed on her back as she laid on her side; Nia knew she was in full-blown labour.

Fernando came into the room, still in his business suit. To Nia, he looked so handsome, despite the nightmare they were living. Given the pain, she tried to muster a smile to show her connection to him and her intent to find courage.

Dr. Caner of the neonatal unit came into the room. His eyes told her the outcome before he had a chance to say the words, "Your baby is too young to survive. You will deliver this baby soon, and we will not resuscitate or do anything other than to make you and your child comfortable."

Tears from her heart and soul streamed down Nia's face. The doctor squeezed Nia's hand to give more of the needed strength to endure this implausible journey. She was unable to speak, so she silently shook her head when he asked if she had any questions. There was no reason to beg and plead for the survival of her baby; the absolute medical decision had been made.

While labouring in the hospital bed, waiting for the in-evitable loss of her baby, Nia reflected on what actually happened to create that horrible situation. Two months prior, she and Fernando were enjoying a beautiful summer day of gaiety at an outdoor family gathering. The sun was warm, and the food, music, and conversation were at their best. That evening, Fernando and Nia celebrated the day with torrid sex, essentially forgetting about the small life growing within her. The next morning, she awoke happy, giving herself a typical morning stretch. While stretching her sore body, Nia felt a tremendous burst from within. Immediately, blood-tinged san-guineous fluid seeped from between her legs.

The phrase "premature rupture of the amniotic sac" haunted her from that moment on. The attending obstetrician had offered a D&C, but Nia refused, hoping for a miracle despite the catastrophe. Eight weeks later, the consequence of their rapture unfolded.

Once the baby's head was engaged in the birth canal, the delivery was quick. With her guilt-ridden thoughts swirling in her head, all that Nia heard was "Apgar of one."

A nurse handed the tiny, pink babe to Nia—a beautiful baby boy. His head moved gently to and fro as he found comfort settling into the palms of her hands. Nia felt his faint cry in the depths of her soul as she put her face to his and felt his thin, translucent skin. She kissed his tiny, perfectly formed body. His face had a strong likeness to his father's. The short-lived sweetness of his baby smell and taste preceded the wetness and saltiness of her outpouring grief. Despite the sorrow, Nia had the mindfulness to use her own tears as the holiest of water to baptize her son with the name David.

In a short time, his tiny crying noises turned to an even fainter whimper, while his colour changed from pinkish to a deeper blue as his last breath faded forever.

Nia's heart wrenched; sobbing engulfed the room. An hour passed, and a somber nurse appeared with a tiny basket. She gently took the baby from Nia's hands, wrapped him in a small white cloth, and placed him in the basket. After one final kiss, he was gone forever.

Fernando couldn't bear the situation for another second. This tragedy was bigger than him. He knew he couldn't possibly help Nia when he was emotionally gasping himself, so he left her alone in the silent, sterile room.

Such a brief time of being. Was it worth the immense pain and heartbreak? Absolutely, was her unshakable answer to herself. She didn't regret trying to hold on to the pregnancy. She put it in God's hands, albeit hoping for a different outcome. Nia was not angry with God, the NICU doctor, Fernando, or herself; anger had no place in her grieving heart.

Nia had rightly or wrongly realized her little boy travelled his whole lifetime in five minutes. In that time, David felt his mother's great love for him by the warm touch of her lips as she tenderly and repeatedly kissed him. While he just fit in the palm of her hands, his tiny 252-gram body looked every bit like a newborn with ten little fingers and ten little toes. He felt the warm tears splash on his tiny chest. Nia imagined that they must've felt like sea waves on his small body. Despite this, David's spirit rallied with all its might to breathe and reach for his mother's face so warm and wet with grief.

Even though her heart was aching, Nia had no regrets. Nia, then and thereafter, cherished this birth and the humanity of a mother and her child, no matter the duration of their physical time together. Nia knew her baby suffered a catastrophe in her womb and struggled to survive as long as he possibly could. David had a natural birth and death. He travelled from fetus to babe, from young human being to old, in one brief interval of time.

Nia knew David's life would never be forgotten. She found peace in knowing his life mattered, and he fought a good fight. Only five minutes can be a precious lifetime to be treasured— never misplaced or forgotten. Despite her son only having an Apgar of one (ten being fully viable), Nia felt gifted by the life experience of gratitude, grace, and peace he brought to her.

Monique and Flynn never heard of David's birth. Fernando downplayed the whole event to his parents: "Nia had a miscarriage. She's fine." The strong undertone of his message was not to mention it again.

CHAPTER 34
NIA GIVES BIRTH AGAIN

By some absolute miracle, one year later, Nia and Fernando had a beautiful baby girl. Nia breathed a huge sigh of relief when she heard her baby cry, immediately followed by "Apgar of ten."

Their baby girl was truly exquisite. Nia and Fernando were over the moon with delight, as were the grandparents, Maria and Carlos. Aviana was thrilled to call her Grandma Monique and her Papa Flynn and tell them they had another granddaughter named Isabella. Monique and Flynn were happy about the birth and pleased to have been spared the worry of the pregnancy.

Isabella was such a happy baby. She quickly became the little entertainer of the family with every cute thing she would do: from blowing little spit bubbles while she peacefully slept to smiling at her big brother Andrew while he made funny faces. Aviana was always singing to her little sister. It seemed like such a long time since joy and harmony existed under their roof.

Despite all of the wonderful family love and attention, Isabella's favourite person was her Mommy. She seemed to glow more in her mother's arms while suckling her breast.

Nia loved that special time, too. Breastfeeding her babies was one of the most wonderful things about motherhood. Feeding her babies was never a burden to Nia.

Isabella quickly found her place in a very busy household, and everything was marvellous for two years. Fernando was finally living at ease. His parents were overjoyed with their new granddaughter and made a point of visiting her every day. Maria always brought a meal, which gratified Fernando's belly. His family was thrilled doing what they all loved to do best, and that was to hang out together.

CHAPTER 35
NIA HAS ANOTHER BOY

oing nothing to prevent another pregnancy, Nia was pregnant again at age forty-one and delivered a beautiful baby boy, Mika, in October of 1995. This pregnancy was by far her easiest one, as was the delivery. "Apgar of ten" was conveyed immediately by the obstetrician, and Nia breathed another huge sigh of relief.

By his first birthday, Nia intuitively knew something was seriously wrong with her Mika. He was walking very well; in fact, he ran very fast for one so young.

Mika was a great eater, which seemed to be Maria's measure that all was right with her grandson. (Her benchmark was, of course, her Fernando.) Verbalizations weren't a requirement for Maria. After all, he was a boy. "Boys talk later. He has an older sister who speaks for him," Maria would respond to anyone that questioned Mika's lack of verbalizations.

"Mika's motor skills are so advanced. His communication skills will certainly catch up," the family doctor told Nia at one of their appointments.

Despite trying not to overreact to this unusual lack of developmental progress for her fourth surviving baby, she could not shake the doctor's or her family's under-reaction. Nia decided to wait until Mika was two years old; if he wasn't talking by then, she would insist on referrals to specialists.

"One, two, three, four, ... fifty". Ten minutes had passed, and Nia counted the times her beautiful two-year-old had banged his head into the wall. She was desperately trying to get ready for work, intuitively knowing it is not normal behavior for a two-year-old to bang his head into a wall.

The day of reckoning came. Mika was scheduled to meet with Dr. Hare, a paediatric developmental delay specialist, that afternoon. Fernando picked Nia up from work and then collected their two-year-old at daycare. It had been another difficult day; Mika had bitten a little boy named Jake. The bite was severe; the skin was broken and bleeding profusely. The daycare staff told Nia and Fernando they would be meeting with Jake's parents, and it would be determined if Mika could return.

Nia fretted more about Mika's behaviour as they waited for the doctor. Thankfully, they didn't have to wait long to be called into Dr. Hare's office. The room was large, and he sat behind an executive-style desk with a whole wall of books behind him. He also had several framed black and white pictures of a beautiful woman Nia presumed to be his wife. Nia could feel her impatience rearing its ugly head when she caught herself thinking, *Who cares about the personal side of this man when my son's well-being is at stake?*

Dr. Hare had given no direction as to how the appointment would proceed. It was a painful twenty-minutes—no words were spoken. The white-haired, heavyset man in a bleak grey suit followed the aimless motions of Mika. Nia and Fernando both fidgeted in their respective chairs, wondering if it was their child's behaviour the doctor was observing or the parents.

Mika moved from toy to toy, not really playing with any of them. He didn't seek to sit on Nia's lap. He repeatedly climbed up and down the ramp attached to a traditional doctor's examining table. Not once did Mika use it like a slide in the park. The observation process felt like a scream in silence.

Finally, the highly recommended doctor spoke, "Does he demonstrate any ritualistic behaviours?"

What the hell does that mean? The prolonged silence left both parents feeling somewhat dumbfounded about what the doctor was looking for.

"Well, I can guarantee one of two things for this boy; he's either entirely normal or profoundly mentally disabled," Dr. Hare said flatly.

Devastation simultaneously pierced Nia and Fernando's hearts. They knew their son wasn't "entirely normal." They left the doctor's office heartbroken, with an appointment for the following year.

Nia tenderly put Mika into his car seat. They drove to Fernando's parents' house to drop him off for the remainder of the day.

Nia stayed in the car, knowing she wouldn't be able to hold it together. Fernando gave his mother his cold stare, meaning don't ask me any questions. He returned to the car finding Nia looking lost and afraid. Fernando took a deep breath and put the car in reverse.

Predictably, Fernando's anguish burst. Nia hadn't seen her husband emote since the death of their firstborn. The 99.9% stoic man was crumbling before her. She once again needed to reel in her own anguish to try to comfort the man she loved. Nia watched in silence as his tears flowed steadily, like a faucet running, unable to turn off. The heaving of his chest and the redness of his face looked like he was going to implode.

The long drive back to her work was eerily silent and didn't change when they arrived. Fernando stopped the car, Nia stepped out, and he drove away. Nia waited until he was out of sight before she walked over to a remote part of the parking lot and broke down in utter anguish.

That experience was the first time Nia needed a coping strategy to deal with the degree of pain. Her go-to solution was an urgency to numb. After work, she hit the liquor store to get her fix.

That night, the couple went through the regular motions of the night; neither able to bring themselves to discuss their new reality. Nia didn't feel the need to say to her husband, "See? I was right. There is something seriously wrong with our son." Nia was content with her choice of survival, as her only escape seemed to be numbing. And so, she began dosing herself in small portions of poison—white wine.

CHAPTER 36

AUTISM

When Mika was three and a half, the family doctor finally heeded Nia's demands for a second opinion and referred him to Sick Children's Hospital in Toronto to see a highly recommended Developmental Specialist. Nia needed some resolution, to have a diagnosis to steer them in a treatment direction, to move forward, but Fernando was irritated to have to take a day off work to drive to Toronto.

Although the day was a frigid, windy February afternoon, it was sunny and warm in the car. Mika fussed in his car seat and kept kicking the back of his dad's chair. Fernando was predictably irked, as had become the common state of his demeanour.

Nia prayed she wouldn't have to deal with her husband's anger at everyone and everything. The drive wasn't lending to her hopes—they endured two long hours of his road rage to get to the hospital.

As Nia collected her bag to get ready to get out of the car, Fernando barked, "Not yet. You need to come with me to find a parking spot."

"Yeah, but it looks like we won't find one close to the entrance. Just let me out. Mika and I will wait for you in the lobby," Nia requested.

"NO!" Fernando's response showed his complete lack of empathy. He continued to drive round and round, side street after side street, until finally finding an available spot in a parking lot one kilometre from the hospital.

Mika, quite disheveled in his car seat, was hot, tired, and seemed to also be at his wit's end for having to deal with his dad's temper tantrum.

Nia tried to pull it together for all of them, to no avail. Once released from the car seat, Mika thrashed in Nia's arms until she could set him down to stand on the cold pavement. He quickly kicked off his boots, one going directly under the next parked car, unable to be retrieved until the car left.

They were already twenty minutes late for the appointment. Fernando marched towards the hospital, leaving Nia to cope and carry a child insisting on flailing all of his extremities. *Where's God now?* Nia kept asking herself. She was at the mercy of Fernando, who marched ahead in a state of fury and was completely out of her sight. Nia wasn't even sure if they were both going to the same place. Finally, she made it to the hospital's lobby and let her son down to continue his tantrum on the floor until he extinguished his internal storm. Exhausted herself, she knelt to the floor, weeping inconsolably.

Fernando was in the corner of the lobby, observing the strangers trying to assist and console his wife, and didn't move to help. Finally—after several minutes—both Nia and Mika stood and proceeded to the sixth-floor waiting room.

They didn't have to wait long before the receptionist called their name, and she and Mika proceeded hand in hand. Fernando was nowhere around, and Nia felt a sense of relief for that.

Dr. Scholler made her assessment after an hour of tests and measures. "He's autistic. His diagnosis is Classic Autism of the Severe Nature."

Nia sat in silence as the doctor spoke. She was neither relieved nor devastated, but she believed the pronouncement.

The doctor continued by giving Nia some tangible actions to follow up with, referrals to resources, books to read, waiting lists to get on, and a follow-up appointment.

Nia left her office with Mika and finally felt a small sense of relief. She had a diagnosis and a direction to get them all out of the abyss—hopefully.

She found Fernando reading a Time magazine in the lobby, looking perturbed that she had interrupted the article he was reading. Reluctantly, he placed the magazine back on the table and proceeded to the doorway.

Nia picked up her one-booted child and followed her sullen husband on the long trek back to the car. She didn't dare ask for his assistance out of fear he would repeat his earlier performance.

Later that night, when the kids were in bed, Nia went into the study where she knew her husband would be watching a replay of a Stanley Cup game. The only way she could get his attention was to stand in between him and the television.

"Move," Fernando said without raising his eyes off the television screen.

She held her ground.

"Move," he repeated with anger brewing in his tone.

"No, I want to know what we can do," Nia said, desperate to get her husband's attention.

"If you can't cope, you should put him up for adoption," Fernando heartlessly replied.

Nia left the study to find the full, cold bottle of wine in the refrigerator. She grabbed a glass and the bottle and headed upstairs.

Alcohol seemed like her only short-term medication to treat her excruciating pain. The wine wasn't her best friend—even though she was treating it as such. It was her liar, falsely giving her a sense of freedom from autism, from her loveless marriage, and her self-loathing for being a mother unable to be available to love and care for all of her children.

Nia had never felt more alone, existing in a marriage that felt more lifeless than her daily drinking to blackout. Of course, she realized her part in the mess, but she couldn't get off her path of destruction. Drinking became her go-to; she wanted to stay numb. She felt overcome with her challenges and sunk deeper and deeper into alcoholism. Nia's life a lie, and she was being unfaithful to her spirit, which she lost in a heap of empty wine bottles.

When the numbness wore off—as it always did by morning—shame and self-loathing would become the predators of anything worth saving. And so, the days repeated themselves, and the downward spiral continued.

Each morning, she'd awaken with the clear image of a pistol pointed to her forehead, and every morning she desperately longed to pull the trigger. Her only reprieve to that ritualistic hostage-taking image was knowing there would be some leftover wine in the bottle hidden deep in her closet from the night before. She began to call that "breakfast."

CHAPTER 37

NOVEMBER 16, 2008, CONTINUED

"What the hell! Nia, wake up! Turn off the damn car. Nia! Nia! Nia!" Bri pounded on the hood of Nia's car. "Nia, you fool, wake the hell up!" Bri continued shouting demands. She gave up on trying to wake her friend up and moved to the back of the vehicle to pull the towel out of the exhaust pipe. "Nia, don't you or Mika dare die! Wake the hell up, or I'll kill you myself, you poor sad thing," Bri continued with her voice now panicked.

From the intense pounding on the car, Bri could see both Nia and Mika stirring. Relieved, she continued to pound. Bri could see the large bottle of wine and a collection of pill bottles on Nia's lap.

Nia was slowly regaining consciousness. Realizing what was happening, she opened the car door to the compassion of her friend.

"Nia, how could you resort to this? Mika, Mika, wake up, Mika!"

Ignoring Bri, Nia was concerned that if she were to live, her son would, as well.

"Nia, did you swallow a bunch of pills? What about Mika? Did you overdose him?" Bri continued her emphatic questioning.

Nia couldn't remember and didn't respond.

Bri grabbed the pill bottles in Nia's lap and shook them—all had the lids on, and pills were still inside. "Thank God," she said. "Nia, you crazy person, you and Mika would be dead if I hadn't come out to check on the horses. The old farm lady I lease the pasture from called me to tell me a car was parked behind the barn. I came to check out what was going on." There was only a slight element of relief in Bri's voice. "Never in a million years would I have guessed to find you here in such a state. Get out of the car, you stupid ass. I'll get Mika out."

The blast of cold air hit Nia's face like a slap of reality. "Is Mika ok?" Nia could see her son waking up and yawning. He looked around and looked comforted to see his mom, his books, and the half-full bag of Smarties.

Mika pulled his favourite things out of the car and placed them on the hood to resume his happy, pre-carbon monoxide poisoning activities, apparently undisturbed by the unconscionable actions of his mother.

Nia, rubbing her foggy head, had to pull herself together and think of a plan before Bri devised her own. "Bri, I know this looks really bad. Things for Mika and me have been beyond hard. Please don't call 911, please? Mika's ok. See? He's eating his Smarties. If the police get involved, they'll put me in jail or a psych ward. Things for Mika will get much worse. Please listen to me," she begged.

"Nia, you aren't well; you were a few minutes from death, and you almost killed your son. Maybe you should go to the psych ward," Bri said with conviction.

"Bri, please don't call anyone. I promise I'll get help. I'll call my doctor tomorrow, I promise." Nia wholeheartedly pleaded with her friend.

Bri knew all three of them were getting cold. It was seven at night. Mika's return time to CPRI was 7:30 at the latest. Looking at Nia, she could see she was desperately trying to shake off her alcohol and carbon monoxide cocktail. "Ok, Nia, here is the plan, but only if you go to the doctor tomorrow. Promise?" Bri was devising her plan of action.

Nia knew Bri wasn't going to take lies. She made her resolve to go to the doctor look authentic, knowing full well she wouldn't.

"Nia, let's get Mika in the back seat of my car. You get in the front. I will drive you both to CPRI. You'll stay in the car and wave to the staff, so they see you. I'll bring Mika to the door and tell them you feel like you're coming down with the flu. I'll also explain to them that Mika didn't sleep much last night, and that's why he seems tired. Hopefully, they won't suspect a thing. What do you think?"

Nia, realizing this was life, not death, had to think fast to cover her near-fatal actions. "Yes, Bri, that'll work."

Nia felt an immense sense of relief, knowing she hadn't opened any of Mika's or her own pill bottles. The wine bottle, on the other hand, had a healthy dent in it.

Bri wanted to help her friend, and it seemed the easiest thing to do was to take Mika back to CPRI; no one would know otherwise. The staff could clearly see Nia waving and thought this situation unusual. Still, it was a plausible explanation and proceeded to usher Mika in to get him ready for his bedtime routine. This was the only time Nia was grateful he didn't have functional language.

Bri got back in the car and reamed her friend for her unthinkable behaviour. They drove back to her car.

Nia pulled herself together and stepped out of her friend's car. "Bri, you were a godsend tonight. I know I've put you in a very difficult position, and I am truly sorry."

"Nia, you need to get help. You're a sick person, not a bad person. You have a disease—alcoholism. I'm trusting you to get the help you need. Now get back in your car and stay warm until you sober up." Bri was certainly convincing with her reassuring words to Nia.

Nia got back into her car, turned on the ignition, and put down the windows to feel the cold winter air fill her lungs. She flipped open her console and found some gum and a small collection of her music. She picked the Beatles' album, *Abbey Road*, and put on her favourite song, "Here Comes the Sun."

Somehow, the lyrics always lifted her spirits, and tonight was no exception. While singing the song, Nia took stock of the pharmaceuticals and the Disney DVDs and then repacked the items in their appropriate bags. Realizing she wasn't sober enough to drive, she leaned back against the car seat and opened the moon roof. She belted out the song "Here Comes the Sun" to the stars and the horses still munching on the hay.

CHAPTER 38
NIA HITS ROCK BOTTOM

B ri drove to the roadway and blocked the laneway for fear Nia might try to drive her car home. Without reservation, she called 911. "My friend Nia has tried to commit suicide by stuffing a rolled-up towel in her exhaust pipe. I've pulled out the towel; she's conscious. She has pills and alcohol with her in the car and has resisted me trying to get help for her. I'm blocking her car from moving. Please come, please hurry." Bri gave her location and waited only a short while before a police car and ambulance arrived.

Nia opened her eyes, not recognizing her surroundings of pink coloured concrete walls. She was alone in a room and could hear the rumbling of shouting and swearing from unrecognizable voices beyond the closed steel door with a tiny mesh-glass window. Where was she? How did she get here? And why was she here? What happened to her clothes, and how did she get the huge bruise the size of Ontario on her arm? The most shocking realization was that handcuffs retrained her hands to the gurney. It wasn't a night terror; it was real. She could see a clock through the small window: 7:00. She didn't know if it was morning or night, nor did she care.

The night before flashed back to her, and she felt a massive wave of nausea she'd never experienced before. How could she have done what she did? How could she have attempted to take her son's life, let alone her own? Then something happened; an immense calmness came over her. The room filled with sunlight, and she could feel its warmth on her face. She heard God say, "It is alright now. You are safe. I am here. I'm looking after you. You no longer have to fight as you have nothing to fear. Feel my love for you."

In the warmth of the sunlight, she opened her eyes and saw her handcuffed hands in prayer with the sensation of His hands pressing over hers. Without a doubt, Nia could feel His love, forgiveness, and the revival of her soul arousing within her. She felt her whole body lose its tremendous tension of resistance. Her body relaxed, and an incredible sense of peace washed over her.

CHAPTER 39

NIA STARTS ON HER PATH OF RECOVERY

After a few days, Nia found herself in the psychiatric ward. She knew she was in the right place. Nia fully recognized she needed help, that she couldn't do this alone. She felt grateful to Bri for calling 911. Bri was correct in realizing her actions were a call for help. Nia was beyond helping herself. Alcohol had become her master, and she was the slave. Every day, the craving for wine made her submit to its hold on her. She couldn't stop drinking on her own. Nia knew she had to be totally removed from it to start her journey of recovery from alcohol, to find trust in the process, and believe that she was finally on the right path.

Her psychiatric team quickly understood that Nia wanted their help and that she was grateful to be out of her world of chaos. They believed her sincerity, her calmness, and her willingness to trust them.

Dr. Jamison was her assigned inpatient psychiatrist. After reviewing her clinical history and the state she was in at the time of admission, he was surprised to meet the quieted, humble woman gently smiling at him as he entered room 36B.

"Hello, Nia. I'm here to help you. To do that, I need your help. Can we do this together?" he asked calmly and respectfully.

"Yes," Nia responded simply. In her voice, she heard her determination within composure.

"Nia, I know you have been suffering for a very long time. You have so many stressors, a big one being your son, Mika, who has autism."

Oh God, here it comes. She was waiting for it; she was sure that she would be charged with attempted murder, and Nia knew she wouldn't deny it.

"You're safe now. Mika is safe. Andrew is ok, and Isabella is with your daughter, Aviana. You can rest. We'll help you get well," Dr. Jamison said.

What, no police? No handcuffs? Bri must not have said anything about Mika being in the car with me while I was going to kill both of us. Thank God for Bri, she said to herself.

After the doctor left her room, and despite being in the "looney bin," Nia continued to feel peaceful and slept for the rest of the day.

The next morning Dr. Jamison returned and greeted her kindly. "Hello, Nia. I hope you're adjusting here. It can be overwhelming for patients at the best of times. I need to know if you feel unsafe here. It's clear to me that you want to get well. I need to tell you something difficult now."

Oh God, here it comes, she heard in her head, but her body stayed calm while she nodded for the doctor to continue.

"I called your husband. I'm sorry to say he has no interest in helping you. He sounded outraged and hung up on me. It's clear that you don't have a proper support system, so we cannot send you home anytime soon. Are you willing to stay longer?"

"Yes," Nia whispered while she gazed at her hands.

"Good, if you were to return home now, you would quite likely repeat what got you here in the first place, only this time without a pulse."

Nia wasn't distraught about Fernando's response to her suicide attempt. She knew he wanted out of the marriage. He wanted Mika gone, too, and his freedom back. Nia knew that her hospital admission was his ticket out.

Mika was still at CPRI, and Isabella was with her sister, Aviana. Her husband was finally alone and undisturbed.

"Nia, I can see you're not surprised by your husband's unwillingness to deal with you and this hard situation. It's obvious to me that your marriage is a big stressor in your life."

"Yes," she replied again while offering a small smile of acknowledgment.

"Your primary nurse, Victoria, has called your friend Bri, who left us her number should you need anything. She's coming today with some clothes and toiletries for you. I hope this is ok with you. We want to see you out of these hospital gowns. Getting up, showered, dressed, and having regular mealtimes are all part of getting well. We start with the basics here. It's great to see you smile a little bit. That's a good thing." Dr. Jamison stood and walked to the door. "See you tomorrow, Nia."

Nia's renewed faith was working for her. All she had to be was relaxed and ready to receive help. She felt a tremendous sense of relief from not having to try to control anything. Her only job was to get out of her own way and trust the professionals who knew what they were doing.

Bri arrived after lunch with a fancy bag full of new clothes for her. Security had been through the bag looking for anything sharp, with strings or belts.

"Bri, thank you for what you did for Mika and me. You did what I couldn't do for myself, and thank you for not telling the whole truth about the situation."

"Nia, I was so pissed off at you. I couldn't believe what I saw when I drove up to your car. Somehow, my anger quickly turned into a question of how could I help you in this absolute mess. I had to think fast; you were drunk. I knew it was no time to have a rational conversation with you. I had to trust my gut, and that's what I did. You, kiddo, have to do the rest.

Stay here; take advantage of the time to finally find some mindful rest." With her comforting words, true to Bri's clarity of purpose, she left.

Nia finally got up and showered. She felt refreshed using all the fragrant toiletries. After her long, hot shower, she put on her new clothes.

The next morning Dr. Jamison returned. "Well, I can see you are starting to look better."

"Yes, Bri came with a bag full of new things for me," Nia said.

"That's great. I want to reassure you that you are on the road to recovery, and I want you to know I believe in your commitment to our treatment. I also want to tell you that because of your positive attitude moving forward with your recovery, I've made a referral for you to see a physician whose specialty is treating health care professionals with addictions. I hope that's ok with you. I promised we would do our best to help you, and I intend to continue doing just that," he said.

The next day, Nia saw a physician specializing in health care professional addictions, who gave her the confirmed diagnosis of alcoholism. The doctor also explained that it was a chronic, life-long disease that would only worsen over time. The treatment was abstinence from alcohol and all other mood-altering substances. She also recommended Nia start immediately with an AA meeting every day. The doctor agreed to arrange for her to have a leave of absence (LOA) from the psychiatry ward to attend the meetings, plus an LOA to attend a weekly therapeutic group for health care professionals.

By the end of the consultation, Nia felt hugely relieved. She finally believed she had direction and support on how to get out from the bottom of the despair of alcoholism. Nia had absolute confidence and a willingness to proceed to the next step.

The next day, she got her promised LOA to go to her first AA meeting.

"My name is Nia, and I am an alcoholic." As she said these words, she had no sense of shame or remorse; she felt relieved to be with equals living in the solution.

Nia stayed in the psychiatry ward for two months, going to meetings every day. Each day, she felt was one step closer to being more at ease. There was so much compassion and support from the women in the AA meetings. She got a sponsor and started working on the steps.

Dr. Jamison didn't want Nia to return to her toxic marriage. He knew that AA, the doctor of addiction medicine, and her therapeutic group were getting Nia stronger in her recovery.

Nia was discharged from psychiatry on January 15, 2009, and admitted the same day to a residential addiction treatment centre for twenty-one days.

There was still no contact from Fernando, so Nia had to find her own way home from a different city on her discharge day from rehab. His detachment came as no surprise to her, and she just rolled with it—just like she always did. Nia realized her husband and his poor care and lack of regard for her wouldn't compromise her sobriety; she held firm to her intentional path of recovery. And so they lived like complete strangers under the same roof. They spoke no words to each other—Nia just stayed out of his way.

Five months into her sobriety, Nia felt a bit stronger and decided to test the water by stepping in front of him on his way to the kitchen. "I'm five months sober today."

That moment could've been Fernando's opportunity to throw Nia a small bone of encouragement, but instead, he chose to spout harsh words of blame at her. "You're the cause of all of our problems. You let booze take over and ruin everything."

To emotionally protect herself, she had to shut herself down. All she could hear was his anger and his repeated use of:

"You . . ."

"You . . ."

"You . . ."

The pain was too great on that cold day. Finally, she came to terms with the need to put a last-ditch plan together to revive their marriage.

CHAPTER 40
DOES HE LOVE ME?

The marital bed was as frozen as the season. Lying beside Fernando, separated by what felt like the Berlin Wall, Nia had déjà vu of the end of her marriage to Simon. "Do you love me?" Nia asked Fernando, knowing he was not asleep yet.

Fernando knew her pause was waiting for his answer but resisted responding. Nia held her position with the question to him and continued to wait him out. After a painful few minutes, he, by rote, said, "I love you."

By his resentful tone, Nia knew he was just saying what she wanted to hear.

The following night, the stage of the bedroom scenario was the same as the previous night. Nia was giving him yet another chance, perhaps to toss her a lifeline, no matter how frayed. "Do you love me?"

"I love you." He recited the words as if he had rotten fish in his mouth.

On the third night, she asked the same question. This time his anger flared like the weekend before with his harsh daggers of words, all beginning with, "You . . . You . . . You . . ."

Nia couldn't bear his repetitive diatribe of disgust, confirming for her with absolute clarity at the moment that this would be the end of her willingness to hold any value or sustainability to their marriage.

Nia questioned herself as to why Fernando wasn't ending it himself. Over and over in their union, it was evident her husband was in a perpetual state of chronic inertia. With any critical decision put before him, he would avoid rather than put any effort into the choice he obviously found too difficult to make. He would shut down any of her questions or concerns. If the issue at hand didn't involve a home-cooked meal or sex, he didn't want to make a connection.

If Nia persisted with a request, Fernando would resort to abusive anger, which was his superpower over her. Simon used the very same weapon of control. And there it was; she finally recognized the pattern of the choices she'd made with her two husbands. With absolute clarity, Nia was determined to amputate the necrosis out of her life. She set in motion her divorce plan.

Nia knew Fernando wouldn't physically leave the marital home given his inability to move forward. She also knew if he felt pushed against the wall by divorce, he would react with violence. The severing had to be quick; in her previous married life, she learned an effective action and once again changed the locks.

Nia hired a lawyer a few weeks earlier, knowing that this course of their marriage was nearing its end, despite giving him multitudes of chances to resuscitate some life back into their marriage. As in his obsessive hockey world, she had been fouled and made the absolute decision to put Fernando permanently in the penalty box and out of her life forever.

The letter from Nia's lawyer was couriered and arrived at Fernando's office on the morning of April 30th, taking him by total surprise. His rage came deep from the volcano within him.

It required no imagination on Nia's part to predict what his reaction would be. Nia knew there would be no going back.

The letter signaled a change for the better in her life. Nia was grateful for her sobriety, her freedom, and her newfound peace of mind and spirit.

Mika finally got out of CPRI and into a lifelong living placement in his own home with twenty-four-hour care. He proudly called it "Mika House" with a big smile on his face. His constant smile reassured Nia he was happy and content in his new place, with a multitude of activities and opportunities based on his wants and needs.

Nia's new life was far removed from daily crises and fear-based survival. Sobriety and living the Twelve Steps of AA taught her a mindful, peaceful way of living. Fear was replaced by faith, worry with acceptance, and imperfection with unique beauty.

CHAPTER 41
NIA MEETS ARJAN

Nia's life continued to evolve, and she had many rewarding experiences. One that Nia could never have imagined happening in her previous life was her passion for motorcycle riding on a Harley Davidson Road King Classic, no less.

Nia's fervour for riding led her to many beautiful places, experiences, and people. This was especially the case in 2014. Early in the year, she and her riding girlfriend, Barb, had the opportunity to help a family of six children—the youngest was only three—who had tragically lost both their mom and dad to cancer. Barb and Nia came up with a fundraising plan to provide a bit extra for this struggling family. They put their love for motorcycling to good use and organized a gathering that brought over one hundred motorcyclists to the event for a "Show and Shine" good time.

The motorcyclists who attended to help the children enjoyed a weekend of camaraderie, food, music, and prizes. Barb had put together beautiful, large, motorcycle-themed gift baskets to entice the participants into donating. Nia's job was going around with a big jug, asking for donations and selling raffle tickets for the hourly drawing: a two-dollar coin for one ticket and five dollars for three tickets. While Nia hated asking for money, she knew she had to rise to the occasion and put on her (well-worn) big girl pants (chaps).

Aside from her chaps, Nia donned her favourite red-sequined Harley Davidson tee shirt, her black leather Harley vest, and her well-traveled Harley boots. Like her mother, Nia had become a confident beauty and celebrated herself with classic red lipstick and Dior's Poison perfume. She loved stepping into her edgy and playful persona, giving the image of a chic, badass biker to raise a lot of money for the orphaned kids.

Despite Nia's disdain for asking people for money, she found herself enjoying the experience. A tall and very handsome man entered the venue looking for Barb, who had invited him. At first glance, he looked out of place; he was older and dressed like he should've been on a golf course rather than a rowdy motorcycle event. The stranger's friendly, confident look captured Nia's attention. His turquoise eyes were like high-beam lures. He sat down with a warm smile on his face, assessing the lay of the land.

Nia saw this as her opportunity to say hello and present her jug. Without hesitation, he donated one hundred dollars. Nia gave him a cheeky wink and moved on, hoping his turquoise eyes would hang around for a while.

Throughout the day, Nia saw him across the room, enjoying the music and the robust atmosphere. As the afternoon went on, Nia was stirred by the man's sincere compassion toward the kids—he didn't try to conceal the tears when he saw orphans' stoic little faces. At that moment, Nia felt an abundance of love for the man before she even knew his name.

The event was a complete success. In just three short hours, the generous motorcyclists raised two thousand dollars for the family of six. The man with the turquoise eyes donated several crisp one-hundred-dollar bills alone.

With the music still pumping and her money hustle completed, Nia wanted to relax a little and enjoy the festivities. The first order of business was to refresh herself in the ladies' room.

Her show-stopping smile needed only a slight touching up of lipstick, affirming she was still rocking the chic biker image she loved. Naturally, Nia wanted to investigate Mr. Turquoise Eyes further while expressing her gratitude for his generosity. She proceeded to strut her badass self to his table of friends, of which Barb was one of them.

"Hi, my name is Nia. I just wanted to thank you for your wonderful generosity toward these kids. May I give you a little kiss on the cheek?"

Predictability, he responded with delight as she laid her ruby lips on his right cheekbone. He appeared enchanted with Nia, declining her offer to wipe off the lipstick mark. "Hi, I'm Arjan. Would you like to join us?" Arjan stood to pull out the chair beside him for Nia to occupy. "You did a great job. Those kids left very happy. It was worth it just to see their little faces light up like a Christmas tree," he said as Nia sat her tired, leather-clad butt down beside him.

"Yes, it certainly was worth it. I find it difficult to ask people for money. Thank you for making it easy for me," Nia replied.

"Can I get you a drink?" he asked.

"Yes, thank you. Club Soda and lime, please. You don't look like a biker guy. Are you?"

"I'm not, but I do ride a bicycle," he said with a glint in his eye.

"What made you want to attend this motorcycle gig?" Nia asked with genuine curiosity.

"A neighbour from my cottage in Parry Sound invited me to join her." Arjan motioned towards the woman seated on the other side of him. "Meet my friend, Janet. She's friends with Barb. Janet felt I needed to break loose and get out of my rut. The ink on my divorce papers is still wet."

"Happy you could come, and I am pleased to meet you," Nia said with a genuine, heart-warming smile.

The afternoon turned into early evening, and the conversation and laughter between Nia and Arjan continued seamlessly. His name suited his grandeur. They discovered that they had many things in common: four children, twice married, a love of nature, travel, fine dining, and theatre. The two had a mutual spirit for adventure, resilience when faced with adversity, and both were Catholic (Nia practically heard a hallelujah from her mother in heaven). The most interesting commonality seemed to be a mutual desire to pursue the joys yet to be found in the remainder of their lives.

As the stars began appearing, Nia said, "This fundraiser exhausted me, and I still have a long ride home."

"Can I call you sometime to go out for dinner or a movie or both?" Arjan seemed anxious not to lose their newly found connection.

Nia smiled and reached into her bag for lipstick. She wrote her phone number on his bar napkin. She knew she had a pen but preferred to play the cheeky lady to the end.

Thoughts of Arjan swirled in her mind on her ride home, and Nia was confident she would hear from him soon. Once home, she peeled off her leathers and gratefully sunk into the bathtub, soaking in the delights of the day.

A few days later, Arjan called her. "Hi, I was hoping to take you out to dinner. Would Friday night work for you?"

Nia knew Arjan would be travelling from Kitchener, which was quite a distance away. Despite the distance, he was obviously keenly interested in reconnecting. "Yes, that would be lovely. I would like to see you again," Nia said. After agreeing on a restaurant, Nia hung up, but her smile remained for the rest of the week.

On Friday night, when Nia was pulling up to the restaurant, she saw Arjan waiting outside the front door with a huge bouquet of long-stem yellow roses. What struck Nia immediately were the yellow roses, a favourable and likely direct message from her dear mother from above. Nia could feel even her heart smiling as she stepped out of her black Audi TT in her subtly sensual little black dress with pearls and heels.

"Hello, Nia. These are for you," Arjan said as he handed her the fragrant bouquet.

Nia graciously accepted the flowers and could see from his expression that he was enthused to see her. She could tell by his look that he wasn't expecting to see a classic feminine beauty; she looked quite different from the well-appointed Harley babe she'd been when they first met. "Thank you for the roses. They're beautiful." As she said the words, she could feel the not-so-subtle presence of her mother nudging her closer to him.

The two were ushered to their table and easily struck up a conversation. Arjan told Nia about his first marriage to a woman he deeply loved and was the mother of his four children. She died of breast cancer when she was only forty-nine years old. Nia could see his unabashed feelings in his memory of her and the life they had together. He continued to talk about his two years of being single following her death and the pangs of loneliness that propelled him into his second marriage.

Yikes. Nia felt a sobering chill up her spine; she related his story to her own, caving into the same feeling. Loneliness camouflaged all the red warning flags of both of their second marriages. Both had traveled down the potholed road of believing they could "fix" their respective partners' selfish behaviours. Similarly, blind loyalty to their vows was the mortar that held both of their fragmented unions together—his for twenty-three years. That conversation led them to ponder together if loyalty was a strength or a weakness. Quickly, they both declared "stupidity" and laughed their way through coffee and dessert.

When the dinner date was winding down, Nia thanked him for the lovely evening and the yellow roses. He walked her to her car and opened the door. Again, she kissed him on the cheek, bidding him goodbye with her flirty insignia, and gracefully got into her car.

On Nia's drive home, she was aware of a synergy taking place, different than anything she had felt before. The friendship with Arjan had a natural flow to it. Nothing needed to be steered, augmented, deleted, or adjusted. By allowing herself to "be" in it and let it evolve naturally seemed like a blatantly obvious course of action. She laughed at herself. "Life can be so easy if you just let it be." She erupted into singing the familiar Beatles song out loud to an invisible audience in her car.

The next day, Arjan called Nia. "I know we just saw each other last night, but I would really like to see you again. Are you free to go to a movie tonight?"

Nia's thoughts were confirmed; he most certainly liked her if he wanted to see her again so quickly, and his willingness to drive from Kitchener showed his eagerness.

It was Nia's dating practice not to have any suitors know where she lived. She agreed to meet Arjan at the movies.

Nia and Arjan enjoyed watching Angelina Jolie's performance in *Maleficent*, and both recognized their enjoyment of the closeness and their shared body heat. After the movie, they went for coffee and talked more about their interests, kids, careers, and travels. They never had idle pauses or discomfort; it was as if they were already good friends.

Nia could see he was a man of admirable character with strong core values and a dedicated commitment to them. Their conversations spanned from the more serious topics to ones sparking belly laughter. This was new for Nia; belly-laughter was never allowed in her previous life. She remembered Simon's mean words, "Laughter is a sign of insanity." At that moment, she laughed off that dark memory and vowed it would never have any grip on her again.

CHAPTER 42
NIA'S DISCLOSURE

Two months into their delightful new relationship, Nia began to grapple with the necessity to tell Arjan about her alcoholism. Any sooner was out of the question; her medical issues were on a need-to-know—not have-to-know— basis. Turquoise Eyes had undoubtedly become important and special to her. Arjan needed to know, and more importantly, she wanted him to know. Progressing any further into the relationship and not telling him was going to make her feel dishonest.

On a Sunday morning, Arjan was making coffee for them; he liked serving Nia her first cup of coffee in bed. She needed the coffee to get up her nerve.

Nia waited until Arjan finished his coffee—it was the least she could do to wait until he was fully caffeinated to bring up this topic. She swallowed the last bit of liquid in her cup and took a deep breath while looking at Arjan sitting in a nearby chair. "Arjan, I have something I need to tell you."

Arjan immediately fixed his eyes on hers, trying to find a clue as to what it could be. His racing thoughts were now palpable in the space between them. He went silent, waiting for her to explain.

"It's time I tell you more about myself. I don't often share what I am about to tell you. Only my family and closest of friends know. I hope you realize that I truly value what we have. Out of respect for you and being true to myself, I need to unveil this to you now. I am a recovering alcoholic and have been since 2008."

Silence hung in the air. Nia had prepared herself for Arjan to leave abruptly. She knew he wasn't a reckless man who would fly into a rage. The silence continued as she knew it would. Nia was pleased that he was seriously absorbing the new information. He stood up from the chair, adjusting his white robe, and joined her on the bed.

"Nia, I had no idea of what you were going to tell me. This information has taken me by surprise. Thank you for giving me the time I needed to process it. First, I would like to say thank you for trusting me and trusting us. You're right, I need to know this about you, and I accept and understand your reasons for waiting until now. You're also right that any longer into this relationship without knowing would have felt deceptive. I want you to know one of my first thoughts was to run."

Nia could see he was becoming more at ease by the relaxing of his shoulders and the return of colour to his cheeks.

Arjan fell silent again, and she honoured his need.

"Nia, I'm not going to run. I understand that you're opening the door wide for me to exit, and I thank you for that. What I want to tell you is my heart and my head are telling me to stay. First, my heart feels an even stronger connection to you, given that you care about my well-being and trust me enough to do what is right for me without pressure or prejudice. I have tremendous respect for what you have had to do and what you have accomplished with your sobriety. What I do know is that you're a wholehearted person, and I love being with you. I don't want to run; I want to stay and hold you in my arms and kiss you."

Nia finally exhaled a sigh of relief and sank into his strong arms, feeling his warmth surround her.

They stayed all day in bed, mostly to get their bearings again and steady their course ahead. After a long, hot bath, Nia felt incredibly relieved she was no longer holding something back from Arjan. She loved the way he assessed the situation and made the decision to stay.

Nia could feel her mojo returning, and her playful self needed to jest after the seriousness of the day. She was getting dressed in her ensuite to go out for dinner while Arjan was in the next room doing the same. She found herself thinking of Marilyn Monroe and one of her notable quotes. All freshly coiffed and sensually dressed with, of course, the classic red lips and Chanel No. 5 fragrance, she was ready to spar with her lover again.

"Hey, Arjan, let me tell you what Marilyn Monroe would say; something like, 'If you can't handle me at my worst, then you sure as hell don't deserve me at my best."

Arjan nodded with a laugh while helping her into her coat.

The following morning, Arjan was feeling frisky and wanted Nia's attention. "Hey, wake up. You've got to see this."

Nia could feel his gentle kisses on her shoulder as her slowly awakening self transitioned into a state of awareness to see two morning doves cooing and coddling each other on the patio ledge outside the bedroom window.

Arjan had used the bird's foreplay outside to segue into setting up their own. "Ah, something else has awakened, my love." Arjan rolled her slightly over, maneuvering her to find her lips, ready to wish her yet another good day.

Their lovemaking was synchronized like musical instruments playing harmonies.

Nia relished being able to exude her freedom while her sensuality merged perfectly with Arjan's.

Arjan and Nia continued to build a happy and grateful life together. Intrinsic to the relationship were the many vacations they took. In one year, they were in ten different countries. Nia had never had such opportunities in her previous life. Travel was always something she yearned for. Whether they were on an opulent cruise ship in the Port of Venice or at a grand resort in Bora Bora or wandering the cobble streets of Maastricht, they would always make their little love nest each night.

Nia was beholden to God for finally showing her the path out of her confinements and discontentedness. She was continually amazed at their mutual good fortune to find each other. The little waif from Sault Ste Marie was immersed in equanimity. The life she was living with Arjan was real; once and for all, no fairy tale.

God had hurt her deeply with her compromised childhood, deformities, insecurities, two abusive husbands, a premature baby dying in her hands, an autistic child, and alcoholism. Finally, God was rewarding her greatly. It took Nia a lifetime to find joy in loving and living. She recognized that in her previous marriages, she confused love with attachment. Her "wasbands" were ill-equipped to nurture or encourage her to evolve into her best self. She had no freedom within either marriage to find, pursue, and cultivate her authenticity. Hard, repeated lessons had to be experienced for Nia finally to accept her imperfections and unhealthy choices in both marriages. She needed to acknowledge her part in the failed marriages, and in doing so, Nia transcended into the woman she wanted to be.

CHAPTER 43

NIA FINDS HER HAPPY EVER AFTER

A rjan and Nia had been together for three years when Arjan got down on one knee and proposed to her on the French island of Corsica, gifting her with a five-carat diamond ring.

Nia had always felt a pull toward France, likely due to her mother's family lineage. Arjan knew Nia would be delighted to have their wedding in France. Together, they chose the beautiful village of Orquevaux. It was truly going to be their dream wedding with just the two of them—no family or friends. They didn't want to allow anyone's judgements regarding their decision to marry to interfere with their day.

It was both their third marriage, and Arjan was fifteen years her senior. Family members felt entitled to give voice to their being together. It wasn't all rainbows and lollipops where Arjan's adult children were concerned; they thought Nia was taking advantage of their father.

Orquevaux had a beautiful medieval church and a wonderful chateau overlooking the sleepy village. Arjan handled all of the arrangements before Nia arrived alone in Orquevaux, one week before the wedding date. She wanted time to reflect on her life's journey—past, present, and future.

The following morning, Nia awoke nestled in layers of soft, white linens to the splendour of a Monet painting in her grand chamber. As she gently stretched her legs and wiggled her toes against the soothing bedclothes, she felt a tremendous sense of gratitude. Her first view of the morning sun gently stroked the forest beyond the stream to its waking. The not-so-distant church steeple chimed its six bells of salutation, announcing yet another new day. Never had Nia imagined a morning could be so blissful and peaceful as the one that was before her to embrace.

She continued to linger in her place of gratitude. Just past the seventh bell, the steeple bade the village to awaken with the chiming of continuous bells; she expected this was a morning ritual musical greeting of awakening.

Her purpose in arriving early to the village was to spiritually and creatively delve into her past with compassionate memories of her hugely difficult times. The juxtaposing of the dark times surrounded by beauty moved her to tread gently through her harsh past truths. Nia needed to revisit and free herself from her unmanageable and tragic days as a child, a young woman, a wife, and a mother. She needed to find balance and give a fresh breath to all that was good in her previous days. Her thoughts of good quickly turned to the birth of all her children.

Nia felt the need to espy her unabbreviated self; the good, the bad, the ugly, and the beautiful. It took Nia more than half her lifetime to get to a place of self-acceptance, self-love, forgiveness, grace, and gratitude.

She went to Orquevaux to get married for the third time. This time was different from her previous two. Nia's life lessons had cultivated emotional maturity, giving her the ability to enter into a union as her true, authentic self—a mature, imperfect, and finally, an enlightened woman.

Nia felt like a natural regal French woman roaming the halls and the salons of the chateau's grandeur, imagining all of the holidays, wedding feasts, and celebrations that had taken place under its great roof. She especially loved wandering into the traditional French kitchen, peeking at what the chef was preparing for the evening meal. Chateau Orquevaux was castle-like, as was Queen Nia with all of her imperfections. She liked the familiar ring to that thought. Arjan frequently referred to her as his "Queen."

The following day, Nia pondered the patterns evident in the lives of the women who had great influence and impact on her life and how they interfaced with her own. Monique's resistance and betrayal of her parents' choice cost her the peace and contentment she always desired. Nia's mother didn't have the resilience or mental health to sustain her fortitude. Monique was devoted to Flynn; however, she offered him nothing but codependency. Her God was a punishing God. She broke all the rules with her choice in marriage, and she spent her life trying to make it right with her God. Despite her challenges, Monique's end was graceful as well as beautiful.

Nia and Lily stayed by their mother's death bed. Monique had metastatic tumours palpable all over her failing body. The oncology doctor told them she even had tumours in her heart. It hurt their hearts to witness the brutal reality of end-stage metastatic cancer. At the time, in May 2004, Nia was surprised at the progressiveness of the management of a palliatively assisted death. Monique was hooked up to a pain pump loaded with morphine. The physician intuitively knew Nia understood what was taking place when she said, "Press this button every five minutes." Monique passed gently on to heaven within a few hours, and Nia knew her mother finally was reconciled with her God. Nia also had absolute faith Flynn was waiting for her in paradise with joyous splendour finally surrounding them both.

The next morning wasn't so sunny. Nia crept back to her memories of the multitude of previous mornings where the dreaded feeling of a barrel of a loaded pistol pressed into her furrowed brow. She persisted with her recollection of the pistol mornings, of the fear and fight just short of self-destruction daily. Nia needed to sit in her recalled, self-centred life of an active alcoholic. She needed to reset and refresh her mindset to acceptance and gratitude. Those days would be forever behind her as long as she stayed true to living the Twelve Steps of recovery. The aroma of French pressed coffee and just-out-of-the-oven croissants gently redirected Nia's journey from past to present.

In quiet reflection with her coffee and croissant sitting on the table in front of her, Nia saw with utmost clarity the directions she took with her choices and the resultant consequences in many ways reflected her mother's journey. It was time to give absolute distance to her previous husbands.

Nia had learned so many life lessons about love. She had learned true love and the union of heart, body, and soul can only thrive in a garden well-nourished with a desire to bring one's best, authentic self to the marriage every day. A life partner needed to truly cherish and encourage the dreams, ambitions, spirituality, and creativity of the other while loving fearlessly.

She believed a true love existed for everyone. Nia had to let go of control to find the wisdom in being patient and letting life unfold as intended. She had great clarity of the qualities necessary for true love and no longer believed in true love appearing as in a fairy tale. Following the lives lived with two "wasbands," she finally knew what she absolutely didn't want in a husband.

After being single before she met Arjan, Nia reflected on what she desired in a man. To keep her on track, Nia wrote out fifty-five things she needed in a man if she were ever to think of another life partner. She was happy to pull out her journal with her notations of the fifty-five things from her suitcase.

There wasn't a better place than Orquevaux to reaffirm her long list before her wedding to Arjan. She opened her journal and read the first: "I desire an affectionate man." She knew with absolute certainty she was a woman who wanted passionate kisses and to be lovingly held in the arms of her partner every day. She reviewed her whole list and fell blissfully asleep.

By mutual agreement, Nia knew she wouldn't see Arjan until he was standing at the end of the aisle at the altar in the village church.

Nia approached the church steps and climbed each one with confidence in their love for each other. She opened the door to the church and saw the multitude of villagers who came to witness the Canadian couples' marriage. The crowd seemed to fade when her eyes locked with Arjan's brilliant turquoise eyes. His gaze seemed to be latched on to his queen, who was proceeding down the aisle toward him.

Nia wore a stunning starry-night blue gown with a matching satin suit jacket and crystal buttons, designed by Canadian Sunny Choi. Notwithstanding the exquisite elegance of her wedding attire, she had never felt more beautiful. Nia also felt her mother's approving presence by the fragrance in her bouquet of yellow roses.

Nia continued her walk down the aisle toward Arjan with absolute clarity and a profound sense of love, joy, and enlightenment.

Here comes the Bride Doll, all dressed in twilight.

BOOK CLUB DISCUSSION POINTS

1. Monique and her parents, Adele and Jacque, portrayed the timeless conflict of inter-religious and cultural marriages. Do you feel Monique made the right choice to marry Flynn?

2. Do you believe Monique was being authentic with Flynn when they first met? Was she truly in love with Flynn, or was she mistaking love for emotional attachment?

3. Why did Flynn take several days to decide to get married, and did he make the right decision?

4. What was Simon's superpower over Nia, and what was the origin of it?

5. What red flags did Nia overlook when she began her relationship with Simon, and why was she blind to them?

6. Why was Christophe, Nia's French lover, so important to her?

7. What reoccurring potholes, and what new ones did Nia fall into when she started her relationship with Fernando?

8. Autism profoundly affected Nia and Fernando's marriage. Why was Fernando detaching in Nia's time of greatest need?

9. Assuming every new relationship will have challenges, for example Nia disclosing to Arjan why she didn't drink and why he decided not to bolt, what were the key elements that had already been established and nurtured in their budding new love relationship?

10. If you could tell your younger self three red flags to absolutely observe and avoid in a potential lover, what would they be?

ABOUT THE AUTHOR

Elizabeth Nancy Jansen is an expert in knowing what it takes to find and nurture true love. Through her speaking, coaching, and workshops, she helps people establish the clarity and focus they need to find their love partner.

Elizabeth struggled to find her own path to love. As a young woman, she suffered feelings of not being enough and made many poor choices by living under someone else's values, judgements, and control.

Although she had a full and highly successful career as a health care professional in a directorship capacity, her personal life choices did not have the same fruition.

Today, Elizabeth is a woman fulfilled with an abundance of love. Her purpose is to help lonely people find meaningful, loving relationships with her step-by-step finding true love program.

Elizabeth is living in the "happily ever after" part of her life with her husband Arnoldus in Ontario, Canada.

Connect at   www.elizabethnancyjansen.com
                 www.facebook/groups/nurturingloverelationships

YOU HAVE JUST FINISHED READING BRIDE DOLL

Nia's love journey took the long way, lined with pot holes and detours to find her Arjan. Your love journey does not have to be as painful. Now is the time for you to find your loving life partner.

This is what I know. He is working (just as hard) looking for you.

Shorten your gap (and his) between looking for love and finding love.

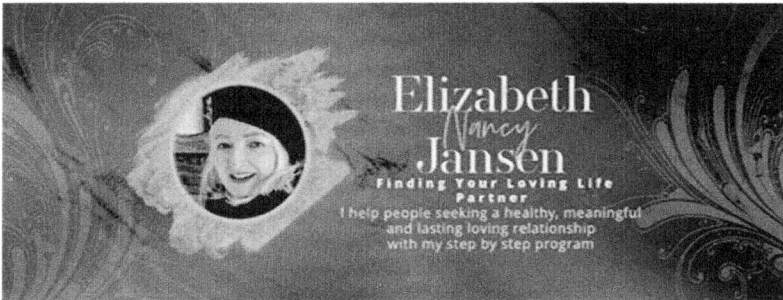

Finding Your Loving Life Partner Program

Formats: One on One Coaching Group Coaching Workshop
Overview   Solution focused, customized for you to shorten
            the gap between looking for love and finding love

- "Reset" from your past

- Customized foundation upon which to build your new action plan.

- Using my step-by-step program with intention, focus and clarity.

- Personalized copyright workbook to keep a record of our epic work together and to share with your new found loving partner for ongoing nurturing going forward.

Benefits   The ultimate human treasure of loving and being loved.

- Greater Health

- Greater Wealth

- Greater Resilience

- Faster Recovery from Illness

- Greater Friendships

- Greater Longevity   (reference: John Gottman PhD of Gottman Institute, The Science of Love)

Love is the only currency of any value in life.
If you are serious about changing the trajectory of
your life to one of alignment with your core values and
desires, then I would be honoured to work with you!

www.elizabethnancyjansen.com
info@elizabethnancyjansen.com
www.facebook/groups/nurturingloverelationships

Made in the USA
Monee, IL
24 August 2021